3

NO ROAD BACK

Wayne R. Boyd

Note for Librarians: A cataloguing record for this book is available from Library and Archives Canada at www.collectionscanada.ca/amicus/index-e.html
ISBN 1-4251-1074-6

Copyright © Wayne R. Boyd 2002
First Published 2002
by MINERVA PUBLISHING CO.
ISBN 1 930493 66 5
1001 Brickell Bay Drive
Suite 2310
Miami, Florida 33131

Printed in Victoria, BC, Canada. Printed on paper with minimum 30% recycled fibre.
Trafford's print shop runs on "green energy" from solar, wind and other environmentally-friendly power sources.

Offices in Canada, USA, Ireland and UK

Book sales for North America and international:
Trafford Publishing, 6E–2333 Government St.,
Victoria, BC V8T 4P4 CANADA
phone 250 383 6864 (toll-free 1 888 232 4444)
fax 250 383 6804; email to orders@trafford.com
Book sales in Europe:
Trafford Publishing (UK) Limited, 9 Park End Street, 2nd Floor
Oxford, UK OX1 1HH UNITED KINGDOM
phone +44 (0)1865 722 113 (local rate 0845 230 9601)
facsimile +44 (0)1865 722 868; info.uk@trafford.com
Order online at:
trafford.com/06-2833

10 9 8 7 6 5 4 3 2 1

NO ROAD BACK

About the Author

The author was born in a hamlet called Greason. When he was about eight years old, the family moved to a farm near the small town of Newville, in south-central Pennsylvania, during the Depression. Like with nearly all the people then, money was scarce as was everything else. But on the farm at that time, the one thing they had in abundance was work.

Growing up, his biggest dream was to be a pilot, which seemed, at that time, quite impossible. Then came the war and everything changed. When he reached seventeen, like millions of seventeen and eighteen-year-olds, he wanted to enter service.

The author was one of six brothers who served in the military during World War II. He entered the Army, and after infantry basic, he was transferred to the Army Air Force. Their unit was attached to the Eighth Air Force, operating in the European theater.

When he returned, he received his flight instructor rating, and worked in that field for many years. After eighteen years with the Air Force in several different fields, he left the government and formed his own business. He is now retired, but continues to fly commercially and for pleasure.

He is life member of the Confederate Air Force with head-quarters in Midland, Texas. It is a paramilitary unit dedicated to the preservation of American combat aircrafts of World War II. It is devoted to perpetuate in memory, and in the hearts of all Americans, the spirit in which these great planes were flown in the defense of our nation.

Chapter One

"Write when you can," were the last familiar words the young man would hear as the train rumbled to a start. It was crowded with people all hurrying to their own destinations. He sat back and looked around at all the unfamiliar faces. Most reflected confusion and fear. As he turned and looked out of the window into the dark night with nothing but a few lights flashing by, he thought, *no single word disrupts and destroys lives like the word war*! We were in it now, and the world and all the people's lives would never be the same again. He thought of his own friends and family he was now leaving; maybe forever. So many young men were going and so many would not return. He thought of his dad and mother standing at the train station. They worked so very hard to raise their large family and now all they could do was stand and watch as the world took them all away, one by one, and now he was the last. He closed his eyes and could still see them standing on the ramp, waving goodbye. His mother was holding onto his dad's arm, fighting back the tears and trying to smile. Tears welled up in his eyes as he thought that they deserved so much better out of life. And he asked himself, *what does it all mean?*

He had tried, since his sixteenth birthday, to join the Army Air Force, but with no success. He was told repeatedly, "We need men in the Army, not the Air Force." One sergeant at the recruiting office convinced him to go into the infantry and while in basic training, try to get transferred over to the Air Force. It would be his only hope. Finally, out of despair, he entered the Army. One day he was a civilian kid; the next, he was ordered to take one step forward, raise his right hand and take the military vow.

The following day he arrived at the training camp and for the next eighteen weeks life would be anything but easy. But he kept asking all his superiors to help him get over to the Air Force. Most just smiled and said only Kilroy would want in that outfit. But he kept trying, not certain he was making any headway at all. He just knew he wanted to fly. It was something he dreamed about most of his young life.

After eighteen weeks it is finally finished. Company "C" which he is part of, is marched to the parade grounds; called to attention, and the shipping orders begin to be read by the company commander. With few exceptions, this company is going to the European Theater of Operations. The last twelve names are called and ordered forward. His name was next-to-last. The company clerk handed them each a piece of paper. They were ordered back into formation and then they were all dismissed. Now it came down to this. He opened his shipping orders and looked first for the destination. The orders read "Kelly Field, Texas". He was now an Army Air Force Cadet.

Arriving at Kelly was not the most exciting thing a cadet should expect. The first week found him on KP. After that, more detailed duty followed. As one cycle ended, the next was being formed. This, he found, was the way it was done; always more waiting. Finally, his orders came. He was assigned to the Flight Training Section of the huge base. Flight officers were assigned to this new group and now the work began. After weeks of classroom work and what seemed like years of study, the men were brought onto the flight line. The flight training was nearly half over, before they received their first weekend pass. They headed to town in little groups. He was with three other cadets. This foursome was soon reduced to just one other fellow and himself. They wandered around town, got something to eat, checked the movie and then went to the USO. Nothing happening there, so they went down the street. They wandered into the 5 and 10-cent store and decided to buy some candy.

"May I help you?" the girl at the candy counter asked. When Doug saw her, he just stood there staring. She was so beautiful he could hardly speak.

He just stammered for a moment and then finally, pointing to a Hershey Bar, he managed to say, "One of those, please." As she handed him the candy, everything went wrong. It fell over the rack and onto the floor. As he tried to reach for it, he dropped his money. Now everything bad that could happen, did. They both scrambled to retrieve everything and in the havoc that followed, their heads bumped.

Finally, she handed him his candy and his change. She still managed to say, "Thank you." He just wanted to run to the nearest exit and never look back. As he went out the door, he couldn't help but glance back to see her again. She was standing there, watching him going out the door and when she saw him look back, she smiled. The rest of his weekend pass was just a waste. He could only think of her.

Then it was back to training again. Another week rolled by and now the word came down that there would be a weekend pass every remaining week of the training cycle. He got his pass after inspection at Saturday noon, and rushed to the bus pick-up point and headed to town – this time alone. He was walking up the street towards the 5 and 10-cent store, not knowing how or what to do to meet her. He walked on past the store and continued onto the square of the little town. He sat down on one of the benches beneath the giant oak trees that lined the street and wondered, *How can I meet her again? She probably thinks I'm an idiot.*

Just then someone said "Hi". There she stood, packages in her arms, with a sort of shy smile.

He was stunned and his heart nearly stopped. "Here, have a seat," he blurted out. She sat down and put the packages on the bench.

"Hi, I'm Douglas Stewart. Just call me Doug. Back home everybody does." With that out of the way he felt much better. The rest was quite easy as he, with a broad smile, asked, "And you are?"

"Lowie Meese," was her quick reply. With that, she took his hand that was offered and held it momentarily and then nervously withdrew as a smile lit up her face.

"And where is 'back home'?" she asked, as she looked directly into his eyes in such a way he could hardly answer.

He heard himself saying, "Oh, a little town in Pennsylvania. You probably never heard of it." "Is this your home town?" he asked.

"It is for now. I'm what you might call an Army brat. My dad is stationed here now. We are originally from Pennsylvania."

"Where?" he asked. "What part?"

"The south-central part. A little town called Zion. It's not even on the map – the state map, that is!"

"I'm from Cedar Hill," Doug said. "That's a town near Philly. You won't find that on a map either. I just can't believe it. You're from the same area back home, and here we are, sitting together on a bench 2,000 miles away. Hi, Lowie, I'm glad to meet you."

They spent the afternoon together and when it came time for Doug to return to base, he held her hand for a long time and then said, "Can I call you tomorrow?"

She gazed up with a soft smile. "Please do."

At that moment the base bus pulled into the curb. He slowly released her hand and said, "Tomorrow." As the bus pulled away, he looked back and saw this beautiful girl standing there, watching his bus drive away. He just knew he had to see her again. Leaning back in the seat he closed his eyes, and all he could see, was this little girl, so beautiful, so warm and tender, with a smile that would haunt him for the rest of his life.

The next day at noon he went to the base theater. After checking the directory, and finding no listing, he caught the next bus to town. When the bus stopped at the town square he got out and sat down on one of the benches. There was nothing he could do, but wait.

After an hour he was sure she had changed her mind about meeting him. Again, he looked down the street, and then looked in the other direction; still no Lowie. He would wait all afternoon if necessary, and even if she didn't meet him he wouldn't give up. Already she was that important to him. He was afraid to admit, even to himself, how much she meant to him.

A few more minutes went by, then suddenly he heard her call, Doug! He jumped up from the bench and ran to her. She was waving her arms and laughing as they met. "I'm sorry Doug, I'm sorry I'm so late. I was with my parents and just got home. I hurried like crazy when I remembered you saying you would call. At the time I forgot about our number being unlisted. I didn't know what else to do but come here and try to find you. I just knew you wouldn't wait all this time."

"Oh! I wasn't waiting long," he said.

"I knew you would be here as soon as you could, but I have to admit I had some anxious moments. Come on, let's get a Coke!" They spent nearly an hour in a soda shop talking, and then she suggested they go to a little park, a few blocks away. Before they realized, it was time for Doug to return to base.

As he went to board the bus, he turned and smiled, "Same time, same place next weekend?"

She smiled and said, "I hope so."

Again he smiled, "I don't think I'll call you anymore!"

She pointed her finger at him and laughed, "You're bad, Douglas Stewart, you just remember where to get off the bus next weekend!"

"I'll be here!" he called back, as he got on the bus. When he found a seat, he looked out of the window and gave her a "thumbs-up" signal. She touched her lips with her hand and turned the hand towards him, as the bus pulled away.

The next day was more training, and the next, and the next. As the weeks added up to months, they spent as much time as possible together. Without talking about it, they both knew what was soon to happen and there were moments of sadness mixed with their true happiness of the times they spent together. Then one evening, when they were walking in the small town park, located on the only hill in the area, they sat down and watched the sun set. They could see far in the distance in all directions. The whole area turned a golden glow. "Isn't it beautiful?" she asked. "Isn't it just beautiful?"

"It really is," he answered. "And you make it even more so." She smiled and took his hand. He looked into her eyes for a long time without saying anything, then softly said, "In a few days I get my wings. Would you come to the ceremony? We have so little time left."

"I know, honey, I know."

As tears started to cloud her eyes she turned her head away and said, "Yes, Doug, I'll be there." They embraced and held each other a long time without saying anything.

Finally he said, "Lowie, I have to go." They turned and took one last look as the sun disappeared. They then started down the hill and back to the town square where he caught the bus back to base.

The next few days were, as usual, very busy. He was now a pilot in all the sense of the word. The final ceremony was all that was left. He hadn't been able to talk to or see Lowie since the evening on the park hill. He couldn't help but keep wondering if she would be able to attend the graduation. He was sure no one else he knew would be there. But then, that wouldn't be unusual, for he was far from home and his friends, just like most of the other fellows there. He just hoped that his new friend would be there, for she meant much more to him than he was willing to admit, even to himself.

They marched out to the parade grounds and stood at attention. As the names were called off one by one, his eyes were fixed on the bleachers. He kept looking for her, but he still didn't see her anywhere. He kept looking as the commander and his aides kept getting closer to him in formation. Now all the men to his right were officially Lieutenants, standing proudly at attention with their bright new wings. It was his turn next. For a long agonizing moment he stood at strict attention. As his vision slowly left the bleachers to near ground level, he felt very sad and alone. Lowie wasn't there. Somehow he just knew she would be; but no, there wasn't anyone to share his happy moment with. Oh well, why should this be any different? That's just the way it was. Tomorrow is another day and I'll be on my way. It doesn't matter. But... yes... this time it did matter. He didn't know why, but it did. His commander quickly stepped in front of him with his pilot's wings and pinned them on his uniform. He stepped back smartly and they saluted. At that very moment his eyes looked beyond his commander and he could hardly keep from shouting, for there she stood on the grass at the bottom of the bleachers. It was, it really was... Lowie. His excitement was unbelievable. For there she stood with the biggest and happiest smile he ever saw.

The rest of the ceremony was just unimportant for him until the commander shouted, "Dismissed." Everyone broke rank and ran to their friends and relatives. He started to go towards Lowie and she came running to him with both arms out, laughing. They fell into an embrace. Then she said softly, "I'm so happy, honey, so very happy and proud of you. I wish this moment could go on forever. I wish... I wish..." and her voice just trailed off to a whisper. "I'll always remember this day. Promise you won't forget me no matter what happens. Please keep this day for me. For no matter how long it is, or if we never meet again, I'll remember you and our day for the rest of my life."

"I know I must leave very soon," Doug said, "and it will be for a very long time. But I promise I'll always remember you and this day and I'll be back. No matter what happens to me or how long it takes. We will be together again. I'll see you back in old Pennsylvania."

They spent the rest of the day together and at four o'clock all civilians were told they must leave the base. They held each other for the last time. Then he stepped back, still holding her hand, and said, "Here is something I want you to have, Lowie." With that, he unfastened the silver wings from his blouse, took her hand, and laid them in it. Holding her hand in both of his, he gazed a long time into her soft eyes and said, "Please keep these for us. It is only a little piece of silver, but it's the only thing I have to give you right now. This is just a little token to remember us, and 'our' day."

"Honey, I couldn't! They're yours. You worked so hard and so long – you can't give them away."

"But, Lowie, I want you to have them."

It was now getting late and he said, "Bye, Lowie – please wait. This war won't last forever and we will win. We just have to win. And I'll survive. Somehow, I'll survive." With that, she hurried to the main gate, then turned and looked for him, but he was gone.

That night the heavy transport planes were taking off to what everyone knew were secret destinations. Lowie heard the drone of the engines and she knew he was gone. In her room she cried herself to sleep and part of her life ended. There was so much to say and do, but it was too late now.

Chapter Two

Doug's outfit arrived at a base somewhere in California, for advanced training in a fighter squadron. Everyone was restricted to base and everything was Top Secret. The schedule was grueling and the training was tough; and after what seemed like years, it was completed.

He was moved to an embark/debarkation area and a day later his shipping orders came through. He was heading to the South Pacific. He was now part of the 239th Fighter Wing, based on a crummy little island that no one had heard of, or even knew existed. As their plane came closer to its destination, all they could see were islands everywhere; islands covered with thick jungles. *Boy! What a spot in the world they picked for me*, he thought. *I guess there are worse places in the world; but if there are, I don't want to know about them.* Their plane touched down with a heavy thud as the pilot maneuvered around some giant holes in the runway. "Well, well," the guy next to him said, "someone knows this field is here. Looks like they don't like it either."

Doug's group was a very small outfit, but their planes were about as good as any in the world. Brand new Lockheed Lightening P-38s. A twin-engine, slim-lined fuselage that made it one of the fastest planes in the world. They were well hidden with camouflage and lined up in a zigzag row. And now they all knew it was time to go to work.

The Wing Commander was Captain Edwards and he had more combat experience that anyone would wish on his enemy, but he always made it back. He outlived two planes and was wounded once. He was awaiting orders for stateside, but those orders just never come.

Captain Edwards called the new men to attention and shouted, "When I call your name, step forward. Malone. Montgomery. White. Adams. Stewart. Lutz. Bosler. Orris." He stood there, looking them over for a while and then said, "Men, this is the last time you will have to stand at attention as long as you are under my command. But don't think there won't be times when you catch hell. You're going to know I can be a son-of-a-bitch. You're going to fly these planes my way; or we're all going to die, and I for one, don't want some damn little Jap killing me." With that he told them to go pick out their plane and get ready to fly a training flight. He would be with them in a few minutes.

They all hurried over to the P-38s and started to choose the one they wanted. Montgomery picked one with a number 22 on its tail. Doug climbed up on the next one, which was number 13. He looked across at Montgomery with a smile and yelled, "How come you picked that one, Montgomery?"

He laughed and said, "It has my age on its tail. Okay, Stewart, why that one?"

"Well, it's sure not my age – but it is my birthday!"

Captain Edwards picked up the envelope on his desk and checked each new man's service sheet quickly. Then he threw them down on his desk, spun around, and stomped out of his hut muttering, "Damn it! All greenhorns!" He walked over to the planes, looked up and yelled, "I see you all have trained in P-38s so I guess you know how to start them anyway. We're going up to 10,000 feet. I want you guys to fall in on my tail like a column, of ducks and follow me; and I mean FOLLOW ME!"

With that cleared, he climbed into his craft which had three blue bars and the number 73 on the tail section. At the cockpit there was an assortment of Jap flags and some Naval craft – even two prints indicating Jap bombers – all of which were official combat kills to his credit. All of these neatly painted on by his ground crew chief, a rugged old Sarge who knew how to keep the planes flying. The captain's voice came crackling over the radios. "Okay, men. Fire those engines." With all engines roaring and the dust swirling around, his plane started to roll to the runway strip.

Everyone checked back to him when they were ready to roll. With that, he said, "Follow me to 10,000 NOW!" They pushed the throttles and one by one, rolled down the runway and were airborne. They all climbed to 10,000 as quickly as their 38s would climb and dropped into a single file behind their Wing Commander. His voice came over loud and clear to each man. "Okay, men. First we do one of these." He yanked back on the controls, climbing straight up and over in a big loop, and before they knew where he was, he said, "Look over your shoulder and I'll take your picture."

Then one by one, they did the same climb and loop, and were again following their leader. He had them up for a long time with no let-up. All in all, it was not a bad practice flight. Finally he said, "Okay, boys, let's go home." They came in one by one; some touching the runway smooth – some with a heavy thud. The Commander thought to himself, *well, not too bad. At least they didn't kill each other.*

The next week was spent reviewing and advancing special combat techniques. They were making as many flights as were possible, never having a chance to do anything but train. Their Commander was on them hard and long, but always fair on criticism and he was noticeably pleased with the results.

Saturday morning the sun came up on a near perfect sky and the men were standing in front of their planes when the Commander's jeep screeched to a stop. He jumped out and yelled, "Okay, boys, let's see how good you really are. Watch me close, because I'm going to try to lose you." He smiled a faint smile, then ran to his plane, and in a few minutes they were all in the air and at it again. The Commander climbed, dived, rolled, spun, and flat-out put his P-38 to its limits; and his men stuck to him like glue. After an hour or more of this, the earphones of the men cracked with the booming voice of their Commander as he shouted, "Okay, guys, let's go home – it's party time."

The dust hadn't settled before the men were all piling on the Commander's jeep. He jumped in and they roared over the strip to the huts. The Commander called the rest of the little squadron together. "Fellows, we're now ready to do the job we were all sent over here to do, but today, we're going to have a party because I have, I think, the best little squadron in this lousy war and we're going to prove it. So break out the booze and food. If the Japs leave us alone today, we're going to celebrate."

It was late in the afternoon when Doug went to his hut. He found some paper and a pen and started to write.

Hi, Lowie,

A lot has happened and I've been under restrictions ever since I last saw you, but now I can write. I don't know how much of this letter will be left after they censor it, but here goes. I'm where it's referred to as "somewhere in the South

Pacific." I've heard of beautiful tropical islands in the Pacific, but this is not one of them. Oh well, there's not much time for sightseeing anyway. Our outfit is small and well trained. My Squadron Commander is Captain Edwards. A real pilot. He has survived a lot of combat. He knows all the tricks and is the best pilot and teacher I could ever have. We all hope they send him stateside soon; before his luck runs out, for if you are here long enough, it will. No matter how good you are, you can't survive this mess forever.

How's everyone back there? It seems so long since I left. I guess it's because I miss you so. You became such an important part of my life, I can't imagine life without you in it. I know your life must go on and I have no right to ask you to wait. But again, I ask you, please wait for me. We can have so much when I get back. Can we go back up reservoir hill; sit on the same bench at sunset and start our real life from there? No matter what happens, Lowie, that's my dream and it's the only dream I have...

The loudspeaker blared over the noise and laughter outside his hut. As he stopped writing to listen, a man screamed, "Fall out. Everyone out! Here comes TOJO's boys again!" With that, he jumped up, not knowing what to expect, and ran outside. Everyone was scrambling in their position. He heard his Wing Commander yelling, "Okay, Rookies. Let's go. Let's get these 38s in the air. Now remember, men, what you have learned. Keep calm and shoot straight. You! Stewart! You're my new wingman, so stay in tight. When I need you, you better be there. Let's go!" They all scrambled to their planes and as the engines came alive with a loud roar, the Commander led the way down the runway and in minutes, they were all airborne. As the powerful engines roared, they all pulled back on the controls and the planes responded with a near vertical climb. In seconds, the small group of P-38s was nearly at the same altitude as the small specks in the distance which they all knew were the enemy planes.

The commander grabbed his mike, pressed the button and said, "Okay, men. Is everyone here with me? One by one now, can everyone hear me? I want to know that all our radios are working. Start with you, Stewart, check in."

"Roger, Commander. Loud and clear."

One by one they all checked back. The Commander said, "Okay, now, we're sure no surprise to those boys today. We see them, they sure as hell see us, so stay close. We're going to make one quick pass...a quick 180°... hit them again... then scatter. Then I'll see you guys on 95° heading in five minutes at 12,000 feet. We'll check for damage, and anyone hurt can merely glide home from there. Now remember, don't shoot without a target." With that, he added, "Here we go! Follow me and GOOD LUCK!" In just seconds, all hell broke loose. There were about fifteen enemy planes, of which at least six were bombers. They made their attack through the maze with machine guns rattling and the planes vibrating, engines screaming. Fire burst out and engulfed one bomber. Another rolled over and went spiraling out of control towards the sea.

Just then bullets ripped through the left wing of Doug's plane. He did a quick roll and dove out of position of a Jap Zero that was on his tail. He pointed the nose of his plane straight down as the Zero tried to follow; but in a few seconds, gave up and pulled out of the dive. Doug slowly pulled back on the controls and lifted the nose of his 38 above the horizon. As the air-speed indicator came out of the red, the plane shot nearly straight up, and the altitude indicator showed 10,000 feet before he knew his position. Just then a plane popped up directly in front of him. He was sure it was within range and he pressed the red button. His machine guns came alive with an explosion. The enemy plane blew up in front of him as smoke, oil, and debris came back over his plane. He found himself far to the rear of the bombers. Just then he spotted some of his group. Pulling into a tight turn, he dropped in tight on the right wing of Commander Edwards' plane. "Welcome back, Stewart," the Commander called over the radio. "Okay, here we go again. See you all on 95° in five minutes. Any of you guys hurt, drop out now." With that, it all started again. The next few minutes seemed like hours. Doug and the Commander's plane were now very close, when a Zero dropped out of the bright sun; only to be met with a hail of machine-gun fire from both planes. Oil splattered over Doug's windshield making it nearly impossible to see straight ahead.

"Commander? Stewart here. I can't see."

"Okay, Stewart, join the rest on 95° ...be with you in a minute... remember 12,000." Doug rolled his P-38 into a steep climbing turn, leveling off at 12,000 on a 95° heading. He throttled back, took a deep breath, then started to check out his craft. Everything seemed okay. There was a little oil coming out around the right cowling, but the oil-pressure gauge was still reading okay.

He pressed the mike button and asked, "Anyone out there? This is Stewart. Can anyone hear me?"

"I got you, Stewart. I'm closing in on your left wing. Over here at nine o'clock. Look over there at one o'clock... three of our guys... see them?"

"Roger, I see them," Doug answered.

"Hey, wait up, fellows. The Commander's not here yet! Let's go home," one of them laughed, "I don't like the company he keeps. Boy, they play rough!"

"Anyone besides me still shaking?" Doug asked.

"Hey, fellow, you don't have a lock on that condition. Just join the crowd," someone answered.

Just then a now familiar voice came over the radios. "Cut the chatter, you guys, and fall in. I'm above you and to the rear, taking a census. Looks like we're all here. Welcome to the South Pacific, your host was the Imperial Japanese government. Nice boys! Okay, let's go home. Any of you guys think you can't make it? Any major problems?"

"Commander, I'm flying a piece of Swiss cheese, but I'll make it," Montgomery reported.

"Stewart here, Sir. I'm losing oil pressure on my right engine, but I'll get this bird back if I have to carry it."

"Okay, you healthy guys, move on out so you can get in and off the runway to make room for us cripples. See you men in a little while." As the first planes touched down, the ground crews came running to meet them. "Hey, not too much damage this time," someone yelled.

"Yeah, but where are the rest of them?" The engines were now shut down and the pilots were getting out.

"Some of our planes are hurt a little," one pilot yelled, "but I think everyone's okay. They're going to be a little late, but they'll make it."

"Over there! Over there!" someone pointed. "Here comes the rest. Clear the runway. Some of them don't look so good." One by one, they made a straight-in approach. And the men watched each one as it rolled by.

"Boy!" one crew chief said, "do we ever have some work to do now! I believe someone got mad at our new boys. Hope you guys are okay."

By now, everyone had shut the engines down and were getting out of their planes and climbing down the ladders. Doug's crew chief grabbed his hand, saying, "Welcome back, Lieutenant. Can I paint a Jap flag on the side yet?"

Doug looked at the Commander and smiled.

"You sure can, Sarge. Stewart gets one and so do a few other fellows. We got four for sure, and one probable... and two were big ones."

"Bettys, Sir?"

"Right you are, Sarge. There's two that won't dump any more bombs on anyone again. We broke up their party pretty good."

They all stood around talking and laughing, slapping each other on the back and then the Commander said, "See you guys in about fifteen minutes in the briefing shack. We'll go over this and see what was learned."

"Boy, what a day," Lutz said, as they all walked towards the shack.

"Yeah," Doug said, "I wish we could all wake up from this nightmare and all go home." No one else spoke until they reached the shack.

As they were about to enter, Adams said, "Think we'll ever make it back?"

"God, I hope so," White answered. "I guess some of us won't, but thank the Lord, we don't know for sure."

The Commander was standing at a map at the front wall as they entered the briefing room and sat down. He turned and said, "Ah, has everyone quit shaking by now?"

"Yes, Sir," Doug answered.

"Good," the Commander said. "Men, this mission was a success. We broke up the raid they had planned on a SeaBee project on down the line. For your first mission, it wasn't too bad. Some of you took too long to turn around for the second pass, which can be disastrous sometimes. You might get caught out there alone when they have another fighter group trailing them, just waiting to pick off a straggler. So remember, stay close and tight. Stewart is my wingman, so don't get ahead of him, but stay close. You will see how well this pays off after a few missions." He went over every detail and made plans and changes for future flights. After an hour or so, he snapped, "Dismissed!"

Doug returned to his own hut where the letter he had started was still lying on the little table. He picked up the pen.

Chapter Three

"Is everything all right, dear?" the lady called from the porch of the small white house facing the base parade grounds.

"Yes, Momma," the young girl standing at the mailbox answered, "yes, Momma, it is now."

"Is that a letter from your young friend? Is he all right?"

"Yes, it's from Doug, and he's okay!" She walked back to the porch and smiled at her mother. "It's the first chance he got to write. He said he started to write but had a little interruption and had to finish this letter later. He says he's somewhere in the South Pacific. It's so censored, it's a little hard to read." She was holding the letter tightly as she walked up the steps to where her mother stood.

Her mother put her arm around her, saying, "You really care for this young man, don't you, dear?"

"Yes, Momma. Yes, I guess I really do."

"Well, good dear, he seems like such a nice young fellow. I'm glad you became friends. This war may not last much longer and then we can all go home again. 'Home'. Doesn't that sound beautiful?"

"I hope you're right, I miss so much the life we had back East."

"I know dear, your father and I both miss it so very much. Someday… someday soon… this will all be over, but until then, if you really care for this boy, let him know how you feel. Write to him regularly, and pray for him often; for what he is going through, we at home will never know. Just pray he returns safely. Pray they all do. We know they all won't make it, but we must continue to hope."

Chapter Four

The crew chief said, "Lieutenant Stewart, they shot up your right engine pretty bad. You were about out of oil. We got it washed down pretty good, but we must change that engine."

"How long will that take, Sarge?" Doug asked.

"We'll work straight through. No breaks. It will be a matter of a few hours and she'll be ready again."

"Thanks, Sarge. I'm sorry to make you guys do all this work."

"No problem, Lieutenant. No problem. That's what Uncle Sam pays us for."

"Yeah, Sarge, I know what you mean. All fifty-plus bucks a month. We'll all be rich by the time this war is over," Doug laughed. "Give me a call when you get her ready. I'll go up and check out your work."

"Okay, Lieutenant, but I can assure you, we give money-back guarantees on all our work out here."

The sun was sinking through snow-white clouds which formed long brilliant rays of bright gold, filling the whole sky to the West. From great heights to the very base of the horizon, a deep blue and (at the same moment) very calm ocean, as Doug lifted his 38 off the runway. He eased back on the controls and started a steep climb. The new engine sounded perfect. He kept climbing until he was above it all, and now was in clear blue skies. He was all alone. After a few snap rolls, loops, and a long sweeping spiral, he leveled off and was again in the golden light of evening over the Pacific. He relaxed a few minutes and looked around. His thoughts flashed back to that sunset in Texas he shared with Lowie. *I wonder if I'll ever see her again*, he thought. He checked his watch. He had been aloft about thirty minutes. It was time to head back as the craft seemed perfect. Back at the base he talked everything over with his crew chief, and thanked him and his ground crew for a job well done. He felt honored to have a back-up crew with the skills and dedication they had. His day ended with a letter to Lowie.

Well, Lowie, it's about three months that I have been here and our small team is working well as a unit. Our commander is the best trainer and pilot I'll ever fly with. I'm sure of that now. Boy, I'm glad I was assigned to his outfit. With his guidance, I might really survive this mess. So much for shop talk.

I was out over the ocean a few minutes ago, all alone, and my thoughts went back to you and our sunset up on the park hill. I really miss you and those few moments we spent together. I hope we can clean up this mess over here soon, so we can all get home. I'm afraid something will happen so that you and I won't ever get a chance to get together; but then, maybe I was assuming too much. You may not want to see me again, anyway. I hope you do, but only time will tell.

All the guys are now painting names and sometimes pictures on their planes. I thought I would paint "Lowie" on mine. Any objections? My crew chief puts some symbols on the side of my plane if I get lucky on my missions. Not too many of them yet, but he thinks we'll run out of space before we leave this place. I told him he'll have to do a lot of the flying if he's expecting that. He just laughed and said that's what the last lieutenant thought, but he had seventeen enemy planes to his credit when he went home. I'm sure I'm not that good a pilot.

Well, I must close for now. Tomorrow comes too soon and it's a little scary not knowing what to expect. It's nine thirty in the evening here now, and I keep wondering what you are doing right this second. You come into my thoughts so often, now. I really miss you, so please write soon and often. I find I'm depending on you more and more as the days go by. I wish I had the chance to talk to you again. We had so little time. I want to tell you so much. I now know you have started a new life for me; a life I hope that will wait for me. Goodnight, and may God be with you.

Doug

Chapter Five

The sun, the birds singing, and the morning haze welcomed her to a new day. It was October, and her life revolved around the letters she received day by day. Sometimes she waited two to three weeks, but when one arrived, she knew it was all worth the wait.

This day she told her mother she would be a little late getting home from work. She was going up to the park on Reservoir Hill to write a letter to Doug. She carried several letters with her all the time and when she sat down on the park bench she started to read them again. After a long time, she carefully folded them; and holding them, she closed her eyes and tried to remember everything of the last evening they spent at this very spot. "Doug," she whispered to herself, "I think I love you. But it frightens me. Your life will never be the same, and I'm afraid I'll get lost in the shuffle." Her hand shook as she started to write. "Dear Doug". She crossed that out and started with, "My darling Doug" but she was a little afraid to admit her true feelings and finally settled on, "My dearest Doug".

Chapter Six

The morning sun broke through a thick haze as Doug walked to the alert shack for the briefing of the day's raid. The Commander was already there, waiting for his crew to arrive. When they all sat down, he said, "Okay men, you have two hours and then we have a small job our boss would like done. Headquarters sent word last night. About 150 miles on down the alley from us, the Japs are up to something. It's not a big operation, but headquarters thinks they slipped in a radio station on one of the little islands. They want us to go down, find it and let them know they're trespassing. Now Stewart, I want you to be the flight leader on this one and I'll be your wingman. One of these days I'm going home and one of you guys will have to take my job and I hope it's soon. I'm getting too old for this damn job."

At exactly 0900 the planes lifted off the runway, picking up a heading of 190°. They climbed to 8,000 feet. As they approached the target area, Doug asked for a check-back on the radios, and told them to follow him in low and fast over the small patch of islands just ahead; and to look for anything that moves or reflects in the sunlight. "Spread out and let's lose altitude right now." With that, he lowered the nose of the plane, and the altimeter needle spun off the altitude in seconds. They were just skimming the ocean. "Over there," Montgomery yelled, "the third island. I saw something! There it is again!"

"It's probably sunlight on glass or something like that," Doug answered. "Let's go in, but don't shoot until we're sure."

"Roger!" Edwards answered. Doug rolled his 38 to the left, scanning the island as he made a fast, low pass-over. He ordered the others to stay off to the north until he made sure there was an enemy installation down there and then – BINGO! There it was! Just off his left wingtip. There were some vehicles and camouflaged equipment. He raised the nose of his aircraft, and with full power, roared up and out of range, calling the squadron to clear their guns and get ready.

"They're down there!" he called over his mike. "We have them in a bottle. Okay, one by one, follow me." He snapped his 38 over on the left wing and went screaming down fast, just over the treetops. He squeezed the red button and fire burst out of the guns bristling out of the plane's nose as the bullets ripped through the foliage below. His Commander followed him through with the next pass and, one by one, they all followed suit. There was some fire and smoke rising out of the jungle as they completed their first pass. Also, they could see spurts of flame pointing towards them. Each one knew the guns below were also in action. After the second pass there was a big explosion, with thick black smoke billowing up. "There goes their fuel supply," Doug yelled. "We'll hit them two more times and then get the hell out of here."

"I'm with you," Lutz answered.

On the final pass, with Doug still in the lead, he saw the place below looking more and more like a junkyard.

And then it happened! There was a loud, crashing sound and Doug's canopy exploded open around him. A piece of debris crashed against his head, blood started to cover his face. He pulled back on his controls and his craft shot skyward. He pulled his goggles off – or what was left of them – and rubbed his eyes. His vision was gone from one eye and the other was just a blur.

"Stewart!" someone yelled. "You okay?"

"I got it in the eyes," he answered.

"Can you see?" the Commander asked.

"Not very damn much, Sir," he answered.

"Someone get in front of me – I'll try to follow you home. I'm going to slow down, this wind is about tearing me apart."

He fumbled around the control panel for the throttle, pulling it back slowly. The craft's speed decreased, his Commander's plane shot by him on his right and then settled in front of him.

"Stewart... this is Commander Edwards. Can you see me? I'm right in front of you."

"Not yet, Sir, but stay close. I might be able to stop this bleeding somehow. Hey, you other guys, keep me straight and level. I'm kind of blind right now."

"Don't you worry, Stewart, we're all here. Just don't you pass out on us. Now, raise that right wing a little. There! Like that. Good. Hold it! Now, a little right rudder... a little more... more... okay there, good! I'll stay here on your tail," Lutz said. "You just take it easy and listen close, okay?"

"Got you, Lutz," Doug answered. The three planes were flying in a straight line with the rest of the squadron off on each side to offer protection on the flight back to home base.

"Hope we don't get any visitors," Lutz called over the radio.

"Cut the chatter," the Commander snapped. "We just want to sneak this guy home. Stewart, is your vision any better?"

"No, Sir, not yet."

"Okay," the Commander answered, "hang in there, we're doing okay so far."

"Lift your right wing, Stewart," Lutz called. "You're drifting off course a little."

"Roger," Doug answered. "I wondered if you were still back there. Commander, my one eye is swelled completely shut now. The other one isn't as bad. Damn it! I still can't see anything. Sorry to cause you guys this trouble."

"No trouble for us yet," the Commander answered. "Besides, you went in first and drew the fire – which saved our necks. As of now, those guys don't have enough radio equipment left to play a Tokyo Rose record."

As the group was making their way back to base, Doug kept wondering how he could get his craft back on the ground after they were at their home base. All the rest of the men were thinking the same thing, but no one would mention it at this time. There was some distance to go yet. Maybe his one eye would clear enough by then. They were still giving him directions in flight when suddenly Doug called over the radio, "Commander, I can see your plane in front of me – not very clear – but at least I can make it out. My one eye is clearing a little. Maybe I won't have to bail out and lose this plane after all."

"You better not ditch that plane, Doug. I'll follow it down, shoot it full of holes and claim it as an enemy Zero," Bosler joked.

The Commander ordered the rest of the squadron back to base as quickly as possible; to land, and then clear the landing area. Doug called his Commander and asked if he could keep someone on his tail for the landing; explaining he would follow his Commander's plane down, and the one following could see everything and give him directions to keep him lined up with the runway at the right rate of descent. The Commander agreed and told Montgomery to stay close all the way down, but to pull up and go around again as soon as Doug touched down. He said, "I don't want three planes destroyed, so let's do this right!" As soon as the rest were down and clear, the Commander, Doug and Montgomery started a long, straight-in approach; each checking back and forth on their radios. Everything was okay so far, but Doug's vision was not improving. He could see very little of the Commander's plane in front of him. He asked the Commander if he would just yell when he touched the runway; then give his craft power and get up and out of the way and he would go on in and do the best he could.

"Okay, Doug, it's your show now. From here on in, it gets tougher."

"I'll listen for your yell on touchdown, Commander, before I start to flare out. The old girl will probably need new brakes 'till I get this done."

"I'm only a few feet above the runway now, Doug," the Commander called. "We're closer… closer… and now… touchdown! Right now! Start to flare, NOW! I'm leaving, Doug. Good luck!" With that, the Commander gave his 38 full power and was airborne instantly. Doug cut the power and his plane settled down on the runway with a heavy thud. He hit the brakes and tried to visualize holding the plane in a straight line. He pumped the brakes a few more times, waiting for the plane to stop. Montgomery, who was still behind him, called over the radio, "You're doing great… just hold her right where you are… Looking good… looking good… that's it! You got it!"

Doug cut the engines and the plane came to a stop. He just sat there and took a deep breath. "Thanks, God! I couldn't have done it without you." By the time he got out of the cockpit everyone was there to help him back to the aid station.

After cleaning the damaged area around his eyes, the medic asked if he had any vision at all. Doug told him, "Nothing out of the one eye, and only a blurred amount out of the other one. Standing this close, Doc, I can't see enough to tell you the color of your hair. What do you think, Doc? What are my chances?"

"I can't say, Stewart. There's too much swelling around the eye area and I don't have the equipment or personnel here at this aid station. But it's something we can't wait and guess at. I'm sending you back where they can do the job. I'm talking stateside, Stewart. So get someone to pack your B-4 bag. You're leaving as soon as I can get you a ride out of here."

"You're the boss, Captain. I'll be ready in ten minutes," Doug said, as he and Montgomery started out the door.

Two hours later he stretched out on the little cot inside as he muttered *damn it* to himself. He was in flight on board a well-used C-47 with several stops ahead before eventually being stateside, probably California. The engines droned on and on and finally he fell asleep.

It was nearly dark when he was awakened by a bump, with the tires squealing as they touched the runway. *Wonder where the hell I am now*, he thought to himself. He raised up to look out of a window, when he suddenly was shocked again to realize he couldn't see anyway. *Boy, this would take some getting used to*, he thought; and for the first time, a brief fear spread over all his thoughts. First thoughts were of Lowie; and then of his folks back home. *I can't let them see me like this*, he thought. *I gotta get fixed up and get back on the job. I can't let those guys down that quick. I haven't done anything in this war compared to the squadron leader.* He felt sorry for him, knowing how long he had been stuck with such a terrible job. *They just have to pull him back soon*, he thought. *He's running out of time. Sooner or later his time will come up. He'll go out on a mission and not return. That's just how quick it happens.*

"Okay, Lieutenant," the Sarge said, "we're refueling and then the next stop is California."

"Sounds good to me," Doug answered.

Chapter Seven

Lowie got off work a little late this day; but it was such a beautiful evening, she started to walk up the hill to the park. Arriving at her favorite spot, she sat down and watched as the sun started to sink below the mountain in the distance. Her only thoughts were how beautiful it was and how much she missed Doug. After quite some time, she prayed for Doug's safety again and then started home.

As she came in the front door, her mother said, "There was a person-to-person long-distance call for you, dear. It came through about ten minutes ago. The operator is going to call back in fifteen minutes."

"Did she say who it was?" Lowie asked quickly.

"No, dear, just that there would be a call back."

"Oh, Mama. It must be Doug! But how? How could it be?"

"Now, don't get upset, dear. We don't know anything yet."

"I know," Lowie answered, "but I'm scared. I love him, Momma. I really do."

"I know you do and I'm happy for you; so let's just wait a few more minutes, it might be the happiest call you'll ever get."

Just then the phone rang. Lowie ran with her hands trembling, picked up the receiver. "Hello!" The operator confirmed the call and then said, "Just a moment."

A reassuring calm voice said, "Hi, Lowie! It's me, Doug."

"Doug! Doug! Where are you? Are you all right? Is everything okay?"

"I'm okay, Lowie. I'm hurt a little, but it's not real bad... honest. They brought me back to 'Frisco. I got some junk in my eyes, and I can't see so good. They're going to operate and they say I should be okay. How are you, honey? I miss you! It's so good to hear your voice. It's only six months, and it seems like years."

"Please, Doug," she interrupted, "which hospital will they have you in?" He went on to explain the location of the Army hospital. With that, she said, "Doug, I'll be there soon. I'm taking the next train out."

"But, are you sure it'll be okay with your parents?" he asked.

"Yes, I'm sure."

"That would be absolutely great," Doug said. "But please don't be frightened. I'm going to be okay as soon as they get their job done."

They said their goodbyes, and as she hung up the phone, she turned to her mother. "Before you ask, dear, you know it will be up to your father; but I'm sure the answer will be yes."

"I just have to go to him. I must! I love him, Mother. I know that now. I really do. He means the whole world to me and I'll do anything to be with him."

"I know, dear," her mother answered. "I've known all along," she smiled.

As Lowie stepped off the train, she saw the base bus and hurried over to it. Once seated, she let out a big sigh, trying to calm her excitement – but to no avail. *I'm actually shaking*, she thought, and had to smile to herself. It was a feeling she had never known and had only read about. Now it was happening to her. *I can't wait*, she thought. *I love him. I really love him. He just has to love me. He just has to! But what if he doesn't?* The thought frightened her. She had to control all these emotions and take it one step at a time.

After quite some time, she was standing at the door of Doug's room. She slowly opened it and saw him lying in bed with both eyes bandaged. After a few moments she found her voice and softly said, "Doug?" He turned his head in the direction of the door and a big smile spread over his face as he said, "Lowie!" Holding out his arms, she ran to him.

"How did you know it was me?" she asked.

"I haven't been away that long," he laughed.

They held each other a long time and then she softly whispered in his ear, "You still won't say it, will you?"

"Say what?" he teased.

"You know what. You still won't say it!"

"Honey," he said; and there was a long silence, "I have never said this before, so I have no practice; but, Lowie, I love you very much and I want to spend the rest of my life with you. Whatever the future holds for me, I want to share it with you. I know it's not fair to ask; but will you wait for me till this is over, and I can come home for good?"

"Darling, you know I will. I love you. I love you. I love you.

You made me the happiest girl in the world and I'll wait – no matter how long. I promise, honey. I promise. Just come back to me."

They had talked a long time when the nurse came in to tell them visiting hours were over and then she smiled and said, "Besides, tomorrow's a big day. The Lieutenant's bandages come off, but don't worry. The doctors are quite sure his eyes will be perfect."

The morning light found a young girl walking on the beach as the waves came rolling in with a loud roar. She was anxious and worried – waiting for visiting hours at the base hospital. Arriving at the hospital a little early gave her time to sit on a bench under a giant tree and just recall what had happened to her during the last six months. A little smile spread across her face as she suddenly felt happy and warm inside, for she knew how very much in love she was and how she wanted to spend the rest of her life with the young lieutenant. A life she knew would have to wait, but one she was more than willing to wait for. She glanced at her watch, it was time for her visit. Now she was really nervous as she hurried to his room. As she entered, doctors and nurses were standing there. She walked in as the nurse said, "Hello, it's all good news." A big smile spread over her face as she saw Doug sitting there – the bandages were off – and he was smiling. He held out his hand and she ran to him as her questions flooded out. "How are you? Is everything okay? Can you see okay?"

"I thought I could, Lowie," he kidded. "But I remember you as a redhead."

She laughed and slapped his arm. "That's okay, honey. I remember you as having just one eye: In the middle of your forehead!" Everyone laughed.

The doctor said, "Well, Lieutenant, as of now you're released. So you are free to report to headquarters. Take care, we all wish you the best."

The sun was bright and the sky was clear as they walked out of the hospital. The air was quite cool and Doug put his arm around her as they walked down the narrow, winding street towards the base headquarters building. "Well, honey," he said, "it's October, but this place doesn't look like the autumn back East. It's the time of year I like best and I really miss it."

"Me, too, honey," she said. "Can't you just see those golden oaks and maple trees now with their bright colors spread out over the rolling hills of the countryside? How I wish we could go back and stay. I miss it all so much; but especially this time of year."

"Someday," he said softly, "someday."

She sat down on a bench outside the headquarters building and waited as Doug went to report in. After a short time he came out with a large envelope under his arm. He smiled and said, "Well Lowie, I don't leave until tomorrow. That gives us tonight and tomorrow. If you can stay, that is."

"I must call home, but I'm sure it will be okay with my folks. After all, I'm a big girl now."

"Yeah," he laughed. "All five feet of you?" She grabbed his arm and held on tight as they walked towards the main gate of the base.

"Let's just spend a quiet night tonight. Tomorrow I'll rent a car and we'll leave real early and drive north along the coast. I hear it's something everyone should see as it's really beautiful. What do you say? Sound okay to you?"

She squeezed his arm even tighter and with a smile said, "Whatever you say sounds okay with me. I just want to be with you now and forever." They caught a cab and went to a restaurant, making their way to a quiet corner where they talked for a long time.

Leaving there, they were surprised to find it was already dark outside. They decided to walk along the beach. Time had passed so quickly and now it was quite late, so they called a cab and returned to the hotel which Lowie had checked into when she first arrived. The hotel was located close to the base and it was quite a distance across the city. The ride gave them time in the cab to plan their next day together. When they arrived at the hotel he walked with her to the door. He unlocked the door and handed her the key. She smiled, and whispered, "Honey, do you want to come in, for a little while?"

He quickly nodded his head, "Yes!"

The morning light was just arriving as Doug pulled up to the hotel where she was waiting. She waved and hurried over to the car. "Hi there Lieutenant. Where did you get this big car? Steal it?"

"Only if we don't return it," he laughed. "Hop in, miss, I'll show you the Pacific coastline. I'm not the best tour guide, but I'm cheap!" She opened the door and jumped in, giving him a big hug and kissed him lightly on the cheek.

"I love you."

"That's the magic word ma'am. Forget the fee – this tour will be for free." As the car pulled away from the curb, their last day together had just begun.

After driving about an hour they stopped at a little country store. The old storekeeper was just opening the door when they walked up the steps. He greeted them with a smile. "You folks are out early – or are you just passing through?"

"We're on a picnic and we need some things," Doug said.

"Picked a great day for it," the old man said.

"We didn't have any choice, sir," Doug answered. "It's the only day we have together – so we'll take it, no matter what."

"Sorry to hear that. Tell you what, son. You and your missey pick out anything you want for your picnic. It's on the house," the old man said.

After selecting a few things for their picnic lunch, the old man walked with them to the car. They talked a few minutes; then the old man shook the Lieutenant's hand, saying "the best of fortunes to you. May you return soon and safe to your dear young lady." He then took her hands and held them for a moment. He looked into her eyes and with a faint smile said, "Though old I now am; I too once had a beautiful lady such as you and with her loving memories I still live. So go, fill the day with your own memories." Reluctantly they said goodbye and slowly drove away. Looking back at the old man who was still standing near his store waving goodbye, she continued waving back to him until he vanished from their view.

A few moments later they turned off the main highway and drove as close to the ocean as possible. They carried their picnic basket and blankets close to the shoreline, choosing a protected spot among the giant rock formations. They had a beautiful view of the pounding surf far below. A short time later they decided to go down to the water's edge for a walk along the beach. As they walked along, they stopped now and then to pick up a seashell or just to hold each other. The breeze was quite cool and there was no one else on the beach. He put his arms around her and held her. Finally, he pointed out towards the sea and softly said, "Honey, tomorrow all of this water will be between us. And God, how I wish I knew for how long. I love you so much. I wish I could tell you just how I feel right now."

She reached up and put her hand on his lips and said, "I know,

Doug. I love you more than life itself. I've thought of this – our last day together – a thousand times and now this is that day. I want to be brave but I'm sorry, Doug, I'm going to cry. Why must this war be in our lifetime? Why can't the world just let us live our lives? It's not fair. It's just not fair!"

His eyes clouded with tears. He softly said, "We're part of the victims of this time in history and I pray to God he gives us the strength to survive. He gave me you for my strength and I shall be forever grateful." They stood near the water's edge in an embrace for a long time with their arms around each other, each with their thoughts of holding back the tomorrow which was rapidly approaching. After walking for about an hour Doug said, "Let's start back to the car."

The waves were starting to roll in on the beach as they climbed up to where the car was parked. As they were having their picnic lunch, Doug turned the radio on in the car and left the door open so they could hear the music as they were watching the surf below. Just then the vocalist began to sing.

Oh, give me something to remember you by when you are far away.

She reached for his hand and held it tight as they listened to every word. As the music drifted softly to an end, she quietly said, "It nearly says it all for us, doesn't it?"

He leaned over and kissed her. "Let's make it 'our song'. From this moment on, no matter when or where we hear it, let's stop and remember us this day."

Her voice trembled as she said, "I promise."

They spent a long time in their solitude, looking down on the big waves rolling in and the seagulls flying so near the surf. It was like a giant painting and they were part of it. "Have you ever been to Mystic Harbor?" Doug asked.

She shook her head, "No."

"I was there once on a weekend pass. I took some training in Massachusetts and went over to the coast to see some of the little fishing villages. It was in the autumn, and the leaves were all turning color. The weather was just perfect. I'll never forget that one little town called Stonington. It was beautiful. We'll go there sometime, I'd like you to see it. If anything should happen to me," he continued, "and you are ever up in that area, drive down to the little pier. You'll see a big flagpole. Just stand there and listen real hard. You'll hear me saying, 'Hi Lowie – I still love you'."

"Please, Doug, don't let anything happen. I'm so scared."

"Me, too," he answered, "me too. We'll need a lot of faith and hope to hold on to the threads of our lives. I just hope you don't get tired of waiting."

"Never, Doug. I'll never stop waiting for you."

The day was rapidly growing old as the sun was beginning to sink closer to the sea. The wind was getting quite cool and they pulled the one blanket around their shoulders, holding each other for a long time. "Must we start back soon?" she asked. He was looking out over the sea and nodded his head, "Yes." She opened her purse and handed a small box to him.

He grinned as he asked, "What's this?"

"It's my little keepsake for you. You gave me your pilot wings. This isn't nearly as important, but I want to give you something."

He opened the box and found a silver ring.

"Read what's inside the band," she said. "I had it engraved."

He laughed as he read, "My General – Doug. Honey, I'm only a Lieutenant."

"Not to me, love. To me you're in a class all by yourself. You're everything in this world that's good for me."

"But without you," he said, "I'm nothing."

She took the ring and slipped it on his finger. "There, you can't take it off till you're one hundred years old," she teased.

"I won't. But you promise to be at that birthday party with me."

"I'll be there," she answered.

"Well, Lowie, we better start to pack and head back to base."

"I don't want to," she said.

"Me neither, honey, but if I miss that flight tonight I'll be locked up in Fort Levenworth forever."

Just as they were about to get into the car they turned with their arms around each other and looked once more at the sea. The sun was now touching the water and reflected skyward with a bright golden-red glow. "It reminds me of the sunsets we shared up on Reservoir Hill. Remember?"

"Forever," Doug softly answered. "I'll remember them forever." He then turned the car around and started south along the coast. She moved over close to his side and he put his arm around her. With her head resting against him, she felt so safe, so warm and happy inside, she wanted these moments never to end. They drove for a long time without saying anything, each wondering how they could let go at the moment soon to arrive. As if thinking out loud, she softly whispered, "I love you, Doug Stewart."

The miles ticked away and now they were back at the base. He stopped in front of the BOQ building, leaned over and kissed her lightly saying, "Be back in a minute." She watched him as he went up the steps and into the building. The total reality of his leaving was now upon her and she wondered how she could bear it. Her new world was in the hands of her young lieutenant. He held her love, happiness and future life in his embrace; for when she was with him, life was complete.

The door opened and he came out with his B-4 bag and some papers. As he opened the door to the car he put the bag in the back, then slid under the steering wheel. He looked at her and said, "I don't want to lose you."

She threw her arms around his neck and started to cry. "You never will, I promise. You never will. I could never love anyone as I love you."

It was now nearly dark. Doug softly said, "I must be at the flight line within an hour. We'll go up to the parking lot and wait there. That way, I can spend the very last minutes with you." Unsure she could answer without crying, she just nodded "yes". A few minutes later they drove into the lot. He pulled up to an entrance gate and parked. They sat there a few minutes without speaking.

Doug finally said, "My flight leaves at nine. Are you staying over, or are you leaving for home tonight?"

"My train leaves at midnight," she answered. "I'll go back to the hotel for my bags and take a cab to the station. Don't worry about me. I'll be okay. I'll cry a lot and miss you every minute you're away, but I know you'll be back someday and I'll be here, waiting for you."

They spent most of their time talking about their future – how she would meet him when he got back to the West Coast. They would get married right away and spend his entire leave time on a honeymoon, slowly traveling back East. She would meet his folks and then they would start planning the rest of their lives. They were so excited about all their plans, they both refused to admit how fragile the threads of life are.

By now, it was quite dark and it was a clear, cool night with a sky full of stars. "Up there," Doug pointed. "See those three stars in a straight line? See which ones I mean?"

"Yes, I never noticed them before," she said.

"Well, of the three in line, I'm going to give you the one in the middle. You can't always find them, but when you do, just pick out the one in the middle and remember me. That'll be 'our star' from now on – Okay?"

"From this moment on," she answered, and gave him a hug. "I'll just say 'hello, honey – I still love you'. This will be another secret of ours." There were just a few minutes left for them. The other men were already starting to board the plane. They got out and he took the bag and papers from the car. They walked to the gate as she held on to his arm as tightly as she could. They embraced for the last time.

"I love you," Doug said. "Wait for me – I'm coming back."

"I'll be waiting here for you," she answered. "Please write often and remember our secrets. They're important things in my life now. I love you, Doug." Slowly he released her, picked up the bag, turned, and ran towards the plane. The engines were roaring as he turned, took one last look, waved back at her, then disappeared into the plane. It taxied down the runway, turned, then started its take-off run.

Lowie watched as it lifted off. With tears streaming down her face, waving as the lights disappeared in the night. The old man that was guarding the small gate said, "Don't cry, missey, he'll come back – he'll come back to you."

Through her tears, she smiled and said, "Thank you, Sir, thank you very much. Goodnight." She turned and started back to the hotel.

The trip back to her home that night was a very sad and lonely one. She sat there, staring out of the window of the train, watching the lights of town and of the scattered homes in the distance, with all her thoughts on Doug; she was wondering how far away from her he was now, with both of them traveling in opposite directions. She looked up at the stars but couldn't find their special one. She opened her purse and picked out Doug's silver wings, gazing at them a long time, she then closed her hand and held them tight as tears clouded her eyes.

Chapter Eight

The heavy transport touched down on a now familiar runway to the young Lieutenant. He let out a tired sigh, picked up his bag and started out the door. Looking around, there were a few changes. He started walking towards the alert shack. Just then a jeep came out to meet him. "Jump in, Lieutenant," the kid behind the wheel yelled. "New here, Sir? Or just a visitor?"

"Neither, Corporal, I'm just returning from stateside. Can't say I'm happy to be back."

"Sorry, Sir, I just got here a week ago, and I sure don't like it." He stopped his jeep at the Flight Commander's hut. Doug jumped out and went in to the Commander's quarters. He was sitting at a small desk with some air charts spread out. As he finished drawing some lines on them he looked up, surprised to see his wingman standing there.

He jumped up and shot out his hand, grabbing Doug's with a strong handshake. "Welcome home, Doug, glad to have you back! I was hoping you wouldn't need a seeing-eye dog. I was a little worried when you left. Your eyes looked pretty bad."

"Everything turned out okay, Commander. It was just some Plexiglas and metal pieces and a hell of a lot of swelling. It took about two weeks but they got them cleared up, and everything's okay."

"How's things stateside? See anything of your folks?"

"No, Sir, but I did see my girl. She came out to the hospital. Best thing that ever happened. After my eyes cleared up, I called her. Her dad is a Major stationed at Kelly, so it didn't take long for her to get there. We had two great days together and we planned our whole future life, starting with our wedding."

"Congratulations, Stewart. I hope it all comes true for you both. I can't wait to get back to my wife. The closer it gets for me to be shipped back, the more I worry the Japs will get me. It's a hell of a way to live. This week has been quiet, but last week they gave us hell. I missed you on my wing, I used Malone, but he's not so good as a wingman, so your old job is waiting for you. In fact, when I leave, I'm recommending you for the Commander spot."

"Thank you, Sir, hope I can do half as well as you." With that, they shook hands again, and Doug left to meet all the other fellows. It was quite a while before he got back to his own hut. He just flopped down on his bunk, stretched out and was soon sound asleep.

The Flight Commander spent a lot of time with Doug the next few weeks; both in the air and at the base, preparing him for the Commander's job. In the process, they became very good friends. The Commander promised to get in touch with his girlfriend and also his folks back home when he got back to the States. As the weeks wore on, the air war wasn't getting any better. On one mission, they lost Malone. Everyone tried to save him, but he must have been shot up bad; for without warning, his plane spun suddenly out of control and exploded on impact in the jungles. It was a tired and saddened squadron that returned to base.

A few weeks later a transport landed and some fellows got off with their gear. One of them went into the flight commander's hut and after a few minutes, the commander came out with a big smile, holding a piece of paper. All of his men crowded around him as he, holding up the paper, said, "Well here it is. They're sending this tired old man back to the States!" Everyone let out a yell as they grabbed him and lifted him up on their shoulders, heading towards the mess hall singing, "Off we go, into the wild blue yonder…" Breaking out the beer, they had a little farewell party for him. When the transport was ready to leave, he signaled everyone to be quiet. He thanked them all for their good work and cooperation and wished he could take them all along back to the States.

He called Doug over to his side, took his cap off and put it on Doug's head. "This, fellows, is your new squadron leader."

Everyone let out another yell of approval; with the usual cracks like, "Glad it's you Stewart, and not me."

Doug shook the Commander's hand and then turned to the men. "We're all going to miss this man a hell of a lot, but we are all so glad to see him get a break. I hope I don't disappoint any of you, and I hope I can do half as well as this man that's leaving us now. I don't know about you guys, but it feels a little scary knowing he won't be here any more."

The Commander interrupted. "You all know your jobs, and you're damn good at it. Just continue to work together, and I hope and pray you all make it back. There were lots of times I didn't think I would, but by golly, I did." They all walked with him to the transport and stood there waving, as the plane lifted off, then slowly disappeared into the horizon.

A few days later Doug's orders came through making him Squadron Commander and promoting him to Captain. Everyone seemed relieved and happy they weren't getting a new commander from another outfit. The transition for Doug and the men worked smoothly.

As weeks and months passed, their support mission and work grew into a heavier and heavier load. Not all the missions were successful. They lost three planes and one pilot. As is customary, Doug, being Commander, had to write that last letter beginning:

Dear Mr. and Mrs. White,

Your son and our close and dear friend was lost on a mission of impossible odds. His courage and flying skill was surpassed by no one. A man of his valor can never be replaced. It is with my deepest regrets I must inform you of this terrible personal loss.

As Doug ended the long letter, he sat there staring into space, then picked up the pen again and wrote:

I remain a stranger to you in a distant land. We hold a common bond and we shall never forget this memory or that bond.

Captain Douglas Stewart

He then started to write again.

My dearest Lowie,

As these months pass by, I miss you more and more. I remember nearly every moment we spent together those last two days in California. They were the best days I have ever had and it's all because of you and the warm glow of love you shared with me.

We had a very bad week here and I just finished a terrible task which is one of the duties a Commander must do. We lost another man and when this happens, the family must be told by someone who was there. I'm sure they will appreciate it as time goes by. It's as I would want it, but no matter how many I write, the task gets harder and harder.

This war seems to just go on and on and there are times when I'm so tired and weary I feel my life is passing as a blur. The weeks just drift into months and I honestly don't know how long I've been here. I've lost track of time and we all feel like tired old men. The destruction and killing goes on and it has increased tenfold since I came here, with no end in sight. Lowie, I pray to God the world that's left will not soon forget the terrible wages of war that were paid by so many, especially the ones who will never again see their homeland.

Lowie, I love you so much. I guess I've anchored my life to the love and the memories we now share. I see our star quite often, as I look for it every night. What I'd give for the night when I'll be holding you and I can say again: "Look honey, there's our star." I received your picture you sent in your last letter. It's sitting here on my desk and to me, you are truly the most beautiful girl in the world. I can still see you standing at the airport gate, waving goodbye as I climbed aboard the plane to leave that last night. One thing I do every night since, is look for our star.

I must stop writing for now, as I'm a little tired and very sleepy. Tomorrow I get three new men, so I'll be spending the next few days working with them. I hope the enemy gives us a little break. We could all use it, and it would give me some time to help the new fellows develop the skills they will need to survive over here.

I was glad to hear you got that surprise phone call from my old commander. I didn't know for sure if he would try to get in touch with you, once he got back to the States. I should have known he would, as he does what he says he will do. He's that kind of guy. I owe much of my survival ability to him. It's tough trying to fill his shoes. I was hoping he would pick someone else as his replacement; but he said I was the man for the job. After six months, we're still doing pretty

good. That's it for now, honey. I'm too sleepy to continue.
I'll finish this a little later. Goodnight for now.

The next morning Doug took the new men on a training mission. After about two hours he wasn't satisfied with their progress and brought them back to base. After some review and a question and answer session, he knew why they were not working out. These three men were right out of flight school. No advanced training at all. *Just what I need*, he thought, *a bunch of greenhorns to train.* He hoped the Japs would let his outfit alone long enough to at least give these poor kids a little help.

After three grueling days, the new men were losing their reflexes from fatigue. That night Doug called them into his hut and told them he was giving them a day off to rest and reflect on what he was trying to teach them. He thought it might be best for all concerned. After dismissing them, he wearily sat down and propped his feet on his little desk, closing his eyes a few minutes. His thoughts immediately drifted back to Lowie and the letter he had started a few days ago. Picking up his pen, he started.

Well, I'm back again. There's been a little break in activities here the last few days, which was good for me, as it gave me a little time to help three new kids learn how to survive this mess. Two of them are good students, but one by the name of Zimm is giving me trouble. He's real cocky and it's hard to teach him anything. One of those who knows more than the instructor. I'm trying everything to get through to him, but I don't have the luxury of time to spend on just one wise guy. I'm afraid he's going to cause trouble for himself or someone else down the line. This kind of pilot is a real headache. Sure hope I have time to change his school of thought.

I hear our song quite often, courtesy of "Tokyo Rose." She plays it nearly every night. I just close my eyes, listen, and live that day all over again with you. There's not much to hang on to over here, but I have an advantage and I owe it all to you. I wrote my parents and told them all about you. I gave them your address just in case. My mother will probably drop you a letter or card from time to time. You'll like her and I know she'll love you. Well, Lowie, I'm getting sleepy and I'm really beat, so I'll close for now. Hoping to hear from you soon. It seems to take your letters forever to get here. Guess I'm just too anxious. Goodnight. Answer real soon.

Doug

After nearly six weeks and several combat missions, two of the new men were blending into the squadron quite well, but Zimm was still a problem. Some of the veteran pilots under Doug's command were complaining to him.

After one mission, Bosler came storming into Doug's hut. "That damn Zimm almost got me killed today! Did you see what he was trying to do out there? He's trying to be a damn hero at our expense. His dad's some politician back in Washington, and he keeps bragging about going back with a great war record that will help him get elected to the Senate. He's nothing but a spoiled brat. I know you are my squadron commander, Doug, but you have to do something about this guy."

"I know my responsibilities, Bosler, and I'm trying very hard to make a fighter pilot out of Zimm, but sometimes a guy like this comes along and it's hell to change them. I already have a meeting set up for tonight for him, here in my hut; and I can assure you, it's not a social affair. If I'm not satisfied with his reaction to our little talk, I'll ground him for a little while, and if that doesn't help, I'll notify headquarters and have them get him the hell out of here."

An hour later, Zimm was standing in front of Doug's desk. He looked up and said, "Have a seat, Zimm."

"I prefer to stand, Sir," he replied.

"Okay Zimm, we both know why you are here. Now let's try to get a few things straightened out. First, I don't want to ever see you pull a stunt like you did this afternoon. You deliberately ran away and hid up there, while the rest of us got shot up pretty bad. Then you dropped down and picked off the Jap cripples that were already on their way down. What the hell are you trying to do! Become a hero at someone else's expense? Now all you have to do is join my squadron and help us do our job and this matter will be forgotten. So, what do you say? Any problem with that?"

Zimm cleared his throat and he couldn't hide how irritated he was. "Commander," he said, "you have only one more bar on your shoulder than I do right now. I'm US Senator Zimm's son and I'm on my way up. So if I were you, Captain, I'd be a little careful how I throw my weight around."

At that, Doug jumped to his feet, and looking him straight in the eyes, said, "Lieutenant Zimm, I'm your superior officer right now; I was sent here to do a job and I don't care if you are the President's son! As long as I am in command, this squadron will do that job, with or without you. Is that clear? Now this conversation is ended, and you, Lieutenant, are dismissed." With that, Zimm spun around and stalked out of the hut.

For the next few weeks, Doug kept Zimm grounded. It gave them both time to cool off. Finally, Doug sent him out on a few reconnaissance flights. Headquarters needed some information on some convoy movements. After a few more weeks, he put him back into the squadron line-up. After a few missions, Doug knew he was fighting a losing battle. This kid would never make a fighter pilot. There was little he could do right now. He needed all the men he could get.

The war kept dragging on and it was now nearly two years since Lowie first met Doug, and her life was centered around her love for him. His love was so reassuring for her. It sustained her when everything else failed. She kept herself very busy, both on her job and at home as well. As the months wore on, she found herself spending more and more evenings up on that hill, either writing to Doug, or reading. It was so quiet and peaceful there and as the sun would set, her thoughts were always of Doug and the happy times they spent there. She had received a letter from Doug's mother introducing herself. It was evident everyone in his family was quite proud of him. She worried a great deal about all her sons as they were now all in service. They were exchanging letters quite frequently now and that in itself was a great help for her. She felt she was truly accepted into Doug's family and there was a great comfort with that feeling. She told Doug in her letters, how gentle and kind his mother was to her and how she looked forward to meeting her and the rest of his family someday.

Three more months passed and Doug had lost another of the original group that made up the squadron. It was Lieutenant Adams. They had served together for over two years. He would be sorely missed, both as a veteran pilot and as a true friend. He didn't tell Lowie any more when he lost a man. He didn't want to worry her or project how fragile their chances of survival were as fighter pilots.

A few weeks later, Doug received orders for what seemed like a very questionable mission. One in which he would have to split his small squadron, sending the bulk of the planes as fighter escorts on a bombing mission of two small islands near the New Guinea area. The Japs had some huge oil and munitions storage depots there. Doug was to use a few planes as decoys by strafing and disrupting a small Jap garrison about two hundred miles from the actual target. The orders were quite clear. Make as much noise and attract as much attention as possible. *Here I go again*, he thought, *playing the game called Sitting Ducks.*

He would take Zimm and Bosler with him, and make Orris the squadron leader to go on to the bombing mission. He would have to take his three planes out well ahead of the actual mission. If the Japs took the bait, he knew the three of them would draw Jap Zeros like bears to honey. What a lousy mission to draw. He wondered if headquarters thought they were Kamikaze pilots. He didn't get much sleep that night. He thought he would wait till morning to tell the other fellows about this gem of a mission. No use giving them worries before he had to.

He got out of his bunk about midnight and decided to write a letter to Lowie.

My dearest Lowie,

I can't sleep too well tonight. It's about midnight here now and I can see our star shining. Remember which one it is? I've been watching it and remembering every moment we spent together. It now seems so long ago. I love you and miss you every day and even more at night. This night is even worse than all the others. I'm really troubled and very lonely. I wish I could tell you just how much love I hold for you. This war seems to be pressing down on me extra hard tonight; due in part to what I must order the men to do in the morning. For the first time I'm really frightened for myself and for my men. I just pray to God that we can all make it back. I'm really uneasy about this mission. I can't tell you about it. They would just censor it from the letter anyway, but darling, I just feel that tomorrow is going to be a mistake; especially for my squadron. I hope I'm wrong, but it's really troubling me now. If things go wrong tomorrow and something should happen, please visit my folks. I so want them to meet you, as you are the most beautiful and treasured gift I have ever received from God. I've told them of my complete love for you and I know they, too, will love you and are looking forward to meeting you. I'm going to take a little break now and walk down to the beach. I'll be back soon to finish this letter so it gets in tomorrow's mail pick-up.

He slowly walked out and down to the ocean. The clouds were dark and the moon would break through for just brief moments. When it did, the waves glistened and they rolled towards the shore. He stood there for a long time. Except for the roar of the sea, there was no other sound. As he stood there looking out over the vast expansion of space and water, he felt so small and alone and it was hard to believe this was all happening to him. How did all these events take place to alter his life so completely? *Here he was*, he thought, *a kid from halfway around the world; starting in a little town in Pennsylvania and now standing all alone on a beach on some little island in the South Pacific at midnight.* It was hard to believe this wasn't just a bad dream. The night was so still; so quiet; and he was really troubled as he thought that in the morning, the war, with all its death and destruction, starts again. As he turned to go back to his hut, he stopped for a moment, looked up towards the heavens and said aloud, "Please God, help us all make it back tomorrow." He then slowly walked back to his hut.

Starting again, he wrote:

I'm back again, Lowie. I went down and stood on the beach for a while and naturally, I was thinking about you, about us, and wondering how much longer we must be apart. Well, love, I better close this letter soon as it's about one in the morning here now and I must be the only guy here still awake.

I wish I could hold back the morning. I hate what I must order these men to do. It's like a suicide mission. I think headquarters is wrong on this one – dead wrong! We're going to get shot to hell and have a bunch of casualties.

I still have that Lieutenant Zimm I told you about. He doesn't make my job any easier. I kept thinking he would take up his responsibility like everyone else here in my squadron. But he won't. He just makes the job harder for the rest of us. On every mission, he always finds a way to avoid making contact with the enemy. It's like my squadron is one plane short all the time. You just can't trust him. Tomorrow, I'm going to make him my wingman. That way, when I split the squadron for this mission, I can take him with me. He'll be like a millstone around my neck, but it will make the job a little easier for my men, and I can keep an eye on him. I swear, Lowie, at times I think he tries to get me killed like I'm in his way or something. I'm sorry that I'm saying things like that in this letter. I never wrote a letter to you like this, but I guess I'm so uneasy about tomorrow. I feel I just have to talk to you about it. Forgive me dear, I don't want to worry you unnecessarily. I'm sure like all the other days, tomorrow will be just another day – it too shall pass.

I send all my love along with all my hopes and dreams of our future. Goodnight, darling. Write soon, and may God be with you now and forever.

Love,

Doug

PS Wait for me, Lowie. I'm coming back to you – someday – I promise.

He folded the letter, addressed the envelope, sealed it and laid it on his desk. It was quite late now and in minutes he had drifted off to sleep. The sun was just breaking through the morning haze as he stepped out of his hut. The gas trucks were already topping off the fuel tanks of the P-38s when the First Sergeant came to give him his maintenance report. "All the aircraft are in perfect shape, Sir. The men put in a lot of hours on them and the line Sergeant guarantees them to be A-1 all the way."

"Thank you, Sarge. Call a meeting of all personnel in half-an-hour, over at the alert shack. Something big is up and I want to talk to everyone."

"Right away, Captain. Will do." Doug went over to his plane to check it out himself.

By the time he got over to the alert shack all the men were standing around laughing and talking and trying to guess what the big meeting was all about. As he approached, someone yelled "Attention" and a hush fell over the group. Just then someone yelled, "I know why you called the meeting, Captain... all our discharges came in the morning mail, right?"

"Wish I could say you're right Corporal, but I can't. So, 'at ease', men, and listen closely. This may be the worst day of our lives for some of us.

"I have the charts and objectives for all the pilots involved in this mission and believe me, it's a son-of-a-bitch. First, I have to split the squadron." This brought a groan from the crowd. "I leave first and take two planes with me. I'm taking Lieutenant Zimm my wingman, and Lieutenant Orris will be your squadron leader for your part of this mission. I warn you men, this is no cakewalk. Some of us may not make it back. Not only are we sticking our necks out, but it's a hell of a long flight. Fuel consumption will be critical; so watch it if you don't want to swim back. After this meeting, I want to go over the whole show with all you pilots, so everyone knows just what's expected of us. After that briefing you may know why I didn't sleep too well last night."

After about half-an-hour, Doug ended the briefing with a special thanks to the ground crew for their extra efforts the last two years. He then thanked his fellow pilots, most of whom were replacements of the original squadron. Only Orris, Montgomery, Bosler and Lutz remained, they had been through many difficult times with him. They had become very close and trusted friends. He dismissed everyone except his pilots. They took a short break and then he called for their attention. "Now, fellows, this is what headquarters has up its sleeve for us. First, I have to split the squadron. I will leave first and I'm taking Lieutenants Zimm and Bosler with me. I'm now making Lieutenant Orris the squadron leader of the rest of the squadron. Yours will be the real mission. There's a big oil dump over in the New Guinea area that the Japs are trying to hide. Headquarters is trying to round up as many bombers as they can spare for a raid, and you fellows are to help with fighter escort. I'm supposed to send three 38s to an area about two hundred miles away from the real target, and make as much noise as possible to draw their planes out of the target area so our bombers can get in and out a little easier. I'm going to take that part of this mission. We three will be leaving half-an-hour before the rest of you."

"Captain…" Orris interrupted, "that's a hell of a ride from here. Fuel is going to be damn critical. If we have to stay over the target area a little while, there's no way in hell we're going to make it back to base."

"Can't argue with that, Orris. That was my first concern, but the experts say they have it figured out with our departure time and flight altitude, we'll have a tail wind all the way. I hope they know what they're doing!"

"Captain…" Lutz cut in "you three are going to be in a hell of a mess of Zeros if they take the bait. How are you going to get out of there in one piece?"

"The theory is, when they find out about you guys, they'll high-tail it back to protect the oil and we can sneak back home. Hey! I agree with you guys. The whole damn thing stinks. But orders are orders – so we'll all go."

He checked his watch. Then he looked over at Lieutenant Orris. "My departure time is 0850 – that's in fifteen minutes. You leave with the rest of the squadron exactly ten minutes later. I want to remind all of you that timing on this mission is very critical if it is to succeed. Thanks, fellows, for your good work in the past and I hope to see you all back here soon. So long. And good luck."

He hurried back to his hut to pick up his gear. Just then the clerk was arriving with the mail. "Here's a letter to you, Captain," he said. It was from Lowie. He folded the envelope and put it in his pocket. He would have to wait until he got back to read it.

He started out to his plane and someone called "Doug!" It was Lutz. Doug waited as he hurried over to where he was standing.

"Why are you taking Zimm with you?" Lutz asked. "You know how he is. I don't trust the son-of-a-bitch. Hell, he's liable to run away and leave you stuck. Let one of us go with you and send him on the other mission."

"No," Doug answered, "I can keep an eye on him and he won't screw up the bomber run. After all, that's what this turkey shoot is all about."

"Well, Doug, you're the boss, but I still don't like it. I hope his

Daddy calls him back soon to the States and gets him out of our hair."

"Don't worry, we'll make it back. Hope all you guys do too," Doug said, as he slapped Lutz on the back. "Right now I have to get my three birds airborne. Help Orris get the rest of the squadron aloft on time."

"Will do, Captain. Take care. I don't envy you."

Doug smiled and started towards his plane.

An hour later, they were well on their way to the bogus target. Everyone was quiet. Doug again checked the charts. Still on course – on time – and all quiet. So far, so good. Lieutenant Orris had the rest of the squadron aloft on time and were well on their way to the real target – the oil dump near New Guinea. Everyone was a little tense, knowing this was one of the largest combined operations they had been involved in. Their rendezvous with the bombers was still thirty minutes away and Lieutenant Orris was rechecking his position. Their air speed was okay – time off was right on – wind was no problem. But he was still worried about forgetting something. They had to be at the right place at the right time. Those bombers needed all the protection they could get. He tried to relax as the engines droned on and on.

Doug checked Zimm's position off his right wing and signaled him to close in a little tighter. Bosler was just to the rear. He again looked over at Zimm, then pointed directly in front of them. A small dot now appearing on the horizon was the island they were looking for, the real target. The plan was for them to skirt it by quite a distance, then break radio silence and attract a lot of attention. This should draw a lot of Jap Zeros off the island. Within ten minutes the bombers would start their bomb run – dropping everything on the oil dump and then everyone scrambling out of the area – hopefully before the Jap fighter planes can get to them. Shortly after leaving the area, the different groups would split up and head to their own bases. Doug and his men would fly a triangle – first drawing the Jap planes off the island to a point due West, and then change course again and head home. If the Japs didn't get to them and they didn't run out of gas, they would live to fly another day. He again checked the time as he muttered, "I guess it looked good on paper, but I still don't like it." He pressed the button on his mike and called Zimm first, and then he called Bosler. "Remember your headings, nail them down tight and stay on them. First we pick up the Japs; then lead them out to sea. Fly that heading approximately ten minutes, then pick up the next heading and start for home. But above all, stay close together."

"Over there!" Bosler yelled. "They see us now! Here comes about a dozen of them!"

"I see them," Doug replied. "Okay, we stay for a few more seconds, and then make your turn. Now start talking about that aircraft carrier we're going to sink – they'll pick us up soon. Good luck, fellows!" Bosler started talking loud and clear about the Jap ship and then Doug and Zimm joined the chatter as Doug yelled, "Okay, change course right now." About ten minutes later what Doug feared most was about to happen. Directly in front of them were six aircraft coming at a near collision course. "Dead ahead!" he yelled on the radio. "You guys see them?"

"Roger," Bosler answered. "What do we do?"

"Don't change course; fly straight through them. They're probably returning from patrol and are low on fuel, so they won't engage us for long, and by now they know what's chasing us. We're kind of in a box right now. The only thing our team has is the best damn planes in the world, and they're about to find that out. In a few seconds we're going to lighten our ammo load. Stay cool and get yourself a few Zeros. Here we go!" With that, he squeezed the button and the fifty caliber machine guns came alive. He rolled a little to his right and picked one plane up in his sights. Again he squeezed the button. This time the bullets found their mark as black smoke started to stream out of the Jap plane. It was rolling out of control as he passed just above it. He nearly collided with another. Quickly rolling to the left, he found another craft in range and fired three or four bursts and then that one exploded. He yanked back on the controls and as his P-38 responded, he climbed nearly straight up to avoid the debris.

"Over there, Bosler! At nine o'clock – two of them are closing in!"

"I see them, Captain. One of them belongs to me!"

"Zimm!" Doug yelled. "Where the hell are you?" There was no reply.

"He's gone, Captain. He's probably halfway to the moon by now." Bosler started firing. One wing of the Zero was ripped off and it started its spin to the sea below. The last Zero in the rear started firing at Bosler's plane, and some of the bullets found their mark.

"My engine is starting to run rough and I'm getting a little smoke in the cockpit, Captain."

"Keep trying to fly in a straight line if you can," Doug told him. "Those Japs in the rear can't gain on us. I sure hope there's no more in front of us."

They flew for quite some time on a straight course and the Jap planes following them were still not close enough to fire on them. Finally they gave up the chase and started to turn back. "Do you think we bought enough time for the bombers?" Bosler asked. "If they stayed on time, I'm sure they are at the target right now. You know this damn diversion of ours might work after all." They were nearly at their last time-fix to change course for home when Doug called Bosler and said he should coax his plane to a much higher altitude. That way, if he had to shut his one engine down and they ran into more enemy planes, he could dive down and still help out a little. "Good idea," Bosler called back.

"I'll stay down here," Doug told him. "But don't stick your neck out too far. Just try to get back to base."

Doug had pulled ahead as Bosler was climbing. There were many broken clouds between them now. Bosler called Doug again, "I'm still climbing; not very fast, but I can hardly spot you anymore."

"Just stay on course," Doug told him. "I'll be down here just in front of you. If you have any more trouble, give me a call..." Smoke came out of his radio as it went dead! A bullet had ripped one of the wires, causing a short circuit. They were now without radio contact. Bosler tried several times to call him, but with no reply. He knew Doug's radio was out. He leveled off and tried to keep Doug's plane in sight. The temperature started to climb on his engine, forcing him to shut it down. Just then he caught sight of another P-38. It was dropping down on the back of Doug. He couldn't believe his eyes! He could see flames shooting out of the nose of the plane. Doug was being fired on! Bosler could see a big red stripe on the tail. It was one of our planes and he knew it was Zimm! Black smoke started to come out of Doug's plane and he did a quick peel-off and dived straight down. Zimm followed, still firing. Then Bosler lost sight of them. "My God! That guy is crazy," he yelled. He knew his only hope was that Zimm didn't know he survived the dogfight and was flying much higher than he was supposed to. With just one sick engine, he would be a sitting duck.

Doug by now was aware of what was happening. He was sure it was Zimm firing on him. He was also sure he could out-maneuver Zimm, but with his engine misfiring, he was losing too much power. He stayed in his steep dive a few more seconds and then pulled into a shallow spiral. He saw the smoke coming out of one engine. He thought he might be able to fool Zimm into thinking he was out of control and spinning into the sea.

There was a near solid cloud cover at a much lower level. If he could make it with no more damage, he might be able to hide from Zimm. He didn't know how serious the smoking engine was. All he could hope for was that it wouldn't burst into flames. He had to make this out-of-control-crash-dive look convincing enough to fool Zimm, before he entered the cloud layer he hoped to hide in. He started to roll his plane as he kept spiraling down. With a blinding swirl he was now engulfed in the thick fog, not knowing how deep the cloud layer was. Doug quickly started fighting to gain control of his plane. With a constant check on the air-speed indicator, he eased the throttle back further and kept trying to stop the rotation of his plane. Finally the instruments started to stabilize and he relaxed his pressure on the controls. The air speed slowed to near stalling conditions and Doug used more forward pressure on the controls, stabilizing the air speed to a comfortable gliding speed. Checking the compass, he settled on a 75° heading.

The oil pressure was dropping on the engine that was smoking and the other one was running very rough. As the pressure approached zero, Doug shut the engine down. He was now left with just one engine and it, too, would soon fail. He started a very shallow let-down to achieve as much distance possible to avoid Zimm spotting him if he broke out of the cloud layer. The minutes ticked by and Doug checked his watch again. It had been nearly ten minutes since he entered the cloud layer and now it was starting to break up. The moment of truth was now at hand. Was he far enough away from Zimm? And could he make it back to home base? He spotted a few small islands off to his right. They were quite some distance off his course, but he was afraid to fly by them with the engine trouble he was trying to cope with. The remaining engine was getting worse. *That's it*, he thought, *I'm going in if I can make it.*

After some more anxious moments, he was close enough to spot what looked like a small beach. "Wonder who owns that real estate?" he said to himself. "Well, look out below – you're getting a trespasser." He started to prepare for a belly landing but then changed his mind. It looked pretty good. "Here goes nothing," he said out loud, as he shut the other engine off and started to lower the landing gear. "Lady, you and I are going in," he yelled and started a straight-in approach. *The sand's looking better and better. Just might make this*, he thought. With the nose of the craft a little high, he started reaching for the ground contact. More back pressure on the controls… a little more… a little more… and then… BOOM! There it was! He pulled the controls back all the way, to keep the nose wheel from making contact. Holding the nose high as long as he could, the soft sand caused the plane to slow its forward speed very quickly. A few seconds later, it came to a full stop and the nose settled down on the front landing gear.

Doug let out a big sigh of relief as he looked around at his new surroundings. *Now to figure out where I'm at*, he thought. Everything was quiet except for the small waves rolling in on the beach. He opened the canopy and crawled out and down the wing, then jumped down to the ground. As he started to walk towards the palm trees, several shots broke the eerie silence around him, as bullets ripped up the sand at his feet. He stopped immediately and slowly raised his hands. Three Japs with rifles pointed at his head came out of the jungle and slowly walked towards him. One soldier was shouting something which Doug didn't understand, so he just stood there with his hands held high. The soldier again shouted and pointed to the '45 Doug had strapped to his side. He slowly lowered one hand and unfastened the gun, letting it fall to the ground. The soldier ran out to where Doug was standing, shoved him backwards with his rifle and quickly picked up the gun. Satisfied he had no other weapons, they started marching back into the jungle.

In a shocked state of mind at what he had just witnessed, Bosler was still flying at 12,000 feet, but was losing altitude as his remaining engine was now running very rough. He knew he needed a lot of luck to make it back to home base. He thought of Doug and wondered if he had survived, or if he had spun all the way in and crashed. His anxieties were closing in on him now. His hands shook as he reached for the throttle. Easing it back to lower the RPMs in an effort to prolong the life of his remaining engine, he tried to think of everything in preparation to ditching in the sea, which was now only a matter of time. The cloud layer was still below him, making it impossible to see what was at the surface. His only hope would be an island someplace. He swore as he thought how bizarre this mission was ending and there wasn't a damn thing he could do about it. Maybe the Japs would get Zimm before he got back to base. Just then, thick black smoke started to stream out of the engine as it started to vibrate, he hit the "kill" switch and the prop slowed to a stop. He eased the nose down to maintain air speed and was now settling fast. In a few minutes, it would all be over. The altimeter was ticking the remaining altitude off, very quickly now. Just then he entered the cloud base and in a few minutes he broke through the bottom and could see the water quite clearly. *Some luck*, he thought, *it's not too rough*. I'll keep the nose high and set her right in – get out damn quick and then hope there are no sharks. "My God!" he shouted aloud, "there's a ship!" He veered towards it, hoping he could glide close enough for them to see him before he hit the water. Just as he flared out to make contact, he glanced at the ship again. Then shouted, "Son-of-a-bitch! It's a Jap ship!" The landing was good; without damage and within seconds he was out and in the water. His life jacket inflated okay and now all he could do was wait. *Sort of between the devil and the deep dark sea*, he thought.

Meanwhile, Doug was led into what looked like a small cave. Once inside, it was quite large. There were several passages leading off from the first large area. His captors shoved him forward and pointed towards the one to his left. As he walked into the passage he could see a door with bars on it and he knew this was the end of the line for him. An officer came towards them and shouted something which Doug didn't understand. And the soldier behind him shoved him into the cell, slammed the door and locked it. "Sweet dreams to you too," Doug yelled.

Chapter Nine

The ground crew were counting the planes as they came in one by one. So far, there were five unaccounted for.

"Who hasn't made it back yet?" Orris asked as he and Montgomery came walking over from their planes.

"The Captain, Lieutenant Bosler, Zimm, Brown, and Connors," the sergeant answered.

"You mean Doug and his fellows aren't back yet?" He glanced at Montgomery – they both shook their heads. "It's not good," Orris said. "They should have been back before us."

"Over there!" someone yelled. "There's one more!" They shaded their eyes trying to see who it was. A few moments later the plane touched down and they knew it was Connors. About ten minutes later another lone aircraft approached. Orris looked at Montgomery. "It's Zimm." Zimm taxied his plane over to their area, killed the engines and crawled out of his plane. As he came over to where the group stood, everyone was searching the skies for Doug and Bosler. But there were no more.

"What happened? Where's Doug and Bosler?" Orris asked Zimm.

"How the hell should I know?" he answered. "We had a hell of a war out there and the last I saw of them, they were on fire, going straight down. I looked for chutes to open, but there weren't any. I had so many Japs on me, I couldn't baby-sit them any longer. I got a couple more and when my ammo ran out, I headed for home. If there ever was a mission above and beyond the call of duty, that sure as hell was it!" With that, he threw his chute on the hood of the jeep, climbed in and told the driver to take him back to his hut.

As he was about to leave, Lieutenant Orris told him to be at the alert shack for debriefing in an hour. Zimm glared at Orris, "Who the hell died and left you the boss, Lieutenant?"

"We don't know that anyone died yet, Zimm, but Captain Stewart put me in charge until he gets back. Lieutenant Montgomery is a witness to that."

"It might be a long time before Stewart gets back," Zimm yelled, as the jeep roared away.

"I don't trust that guy," Orris said.

"You have a hell of a lot of company," Montgomery answered. "I don't think anyone in this squadron can stand him."

Lieutenant Zimm spent the next hour writing his very detailed letter to his dad in Washington. His version of the day's raid was quite different from what, in fact, took place; but for him it was another step towards "hero" status and the attention in Washington he felt he needed.

Lieutenant Orris and Montgomery walked over to Zimm's plane. They looked it over quite well, but were not surprised to find no damage. They checked his ammunition supply and found it as he said – empty. "Well, he used all his ammo," Orris said, "but I wonder on what? Sure hope Doug and Bosler make it back." Orris checked his watch. "They're out of fuel by now. We'll have to make the 'missing' report on them. I'm really getting scared now," Orris said. "I should have gone with them instead of that cut-throat Zimm. He probably ran and hid like he did before and left the other two guys holding the bag. If I find that to be the case, the son-of-a-bitch will never leave this island alive!"

It was nearly dark when Orris called all the men to the alert shack area. He asked them to hold the noise down and then started to speak. "Men, the combined effort of this raid was a real success. But for our little squadron, the cost was too high. As you all know by now, our squadron leader, Captain Stewart, Lieutenant Bosler, and Lieutenant Brown didn't make it back. Our only hope is that they survived and the Navy will pick them up soon. Those of us who have survived know not only have we lost three of our best fighter pilots, but more important three of the best friends we will ever have." As he spoke, tears swelled up in his eyes and it was difficult to keep talking, but he went on to explain he was getting word to headquarters to find out what they wanted to do about leadership and replacement. So far, no answer. With that, he dismissed them and he and Montgomery slowly walked back to their huts feeling more depressed than at any time in their life. "I can't believe they're not back," Orris said.

"God, I'm going to miss Doug's leadership. Think any of us will survive this damn war?"

"I don't know," Montgomery answered. "It sure makes you stop and think." They talked late into the night, making plans for search and rescue missions, starting early in the morning. They knew they could do this much, only until headquarters shipped in the new replacements. If they had no success until then, Doug and the other two would officially be listed as missing in action. This was a thought they both tried to avoid.

Three days later, the new squadron leader, a Captain Dan and six new pilots arrived. Except for the Captain, they were as the planes they flew in – new and with no experience. After a get-acquainted briefing, the Captain asked Orris and Montgomery to take care of personal property of those fellow pilots who were lost. They went to Doug's hut first. After packing his few personal things, and getting them ready to ship back to his home, Montgomery picked up the letter addressed to Miss L Meese. He looked at Orris. "We'll have to mail this."

"I know," his friend answered.

"God, I pity her and I don't even know her. What a rotten way for a friendship to end. From now on, it will never be the same around here, and I guess that will be true of her life too. He was the kind of guy you don't soon forget. God be with you, Doug – wherever you are."

Chapter Ten

"Lowie, there was a letter for you today. I put it on the desk in your room."

"From Doug?" she asked.

"Of course," her mother answered, "who else?"

"No one," Lowie called back, as she hurried up the stairs. She quickly opened the letter and started to read. Just then the telephone rang.

"It's for you, dear," her mother called from the bottom of the stairs. "It's long distance." Taking the letter with her, she hurried down the stairs. Her mother handed her the telephone. She momentarily closed her eyes and then said, "Hello."

"Lowie, this is Doug's mother. I just received terrible, terrible news. I've been informed Doug's plane was shot down and he's missing." With that, she burst into tears saying, "I'm sorry, Lowie, I just can't talk right now. I'll be in touch later." She was crying as the telephone clicked.

Lowie was still standing there holding the receiver – a look of shock came over her face and her mother asked, "What is it, dear – what's wrong?"

"It's Doug. He's been shot down." She started to sob as she sat down on the steps, still holding the telephone. Her mother came over, put her arms around her, and tried to comfort her. "What am I going to do? Dear God, please, not Doug. Please don't take him." With tears streaming down her face, she continued to sob for a long time, with her mother trying to comfort her, in vain.

Chapter Eleven

Two months later and halfway around the world, two men on a small island in the Pacific looked at each other in disbelief as their squadron leader congratulated Lieutenant Zimm on his shipping orders back to the States. He was being called back to Washington for a citation ceremony and the rumors were already spreading it might be a CMH (Congressional Medal of Honor). "Montgomery, can you believe this?" Orris asked in disgust.

"It doesn't surprise me. Doesn't surprise me a damn bit! I told you the guy could never fly a plane. He just knows how to pull strings and go home the hero, and here we are, still stuck in this hellhole! I guess next they'll make him President!"

"Let's get out of here before I throw up," Orris said.

"One thing about it," Montgomery answered, as they walked away, "we won't have to wonder where the bastard is hiding on our missions from here on out!"

"Yeah!" his friend answered. "We'll know he's back in Washington – sticking close to Senator Daddy."

Chapter Twelve

"Stand up, Yankee Dog!" the man shouted as the Jap soldier opened the little cell door. He wore what Doug guessed was a Navy uniform. It was the first time Doug saw anyone in the last three weeks, since the day they interrogated him for six hours; then knocked him unconscious because he refused to give them information they wanted. The guard pushed him out the door with the barrel of his rifle. Doug stumbled, but managed to walk out though he felt weakened from his diet designed to keep him barely alive. The Navy officer led the way down to the beach. As they approached the water's edge, Doug looked for his plane. But it wasn't there. He did see a small sub lying offshore a short distance. The guard shouted "Halt!" and Doug stopped, still facing the sea, with the guard back of him. He wondered if they were now going to execute him. No one spoke. They just stood there. Finally the officer shouted, "Yankee Dog! Point in which direction your base is or he'll blow your brains out!" Doug slowly lifted his arm and pointed towards what he thought would be Australia. "How far you fly before shot down?"

"About an hour-and-a-half," Doug answered. He was sure they had checked his remaining fuel supply but he thought he might be able to string them along.

"Pig!" the officer screamed. "You lie!"

"You use more fuel – I got lost after our squadron got shot up so bad. Your boys gave us hell. I think I'm the only survivor."

A broad smile spread across the officer's face, as he said, "Sooooo – now you Yankee Dogs know you are no match for the fighting men of the Imperial Japanese government. You will all die!" He ordered the guard to return the prisoner to his cell. As Doug walked back, he kept looking for his plane. It was back in the jungle quite a distance. They had cut the trees and moved it back from the beach. It now stood completely camouflaged. Spotting it from the air would be nearly impossible. Doug's hope of rescue was now, he was sure, just a dream.

Every day they would drag him from the cell and beat him when he wouldn't answer their repeated questions. As the months passed, his condition kept getting worse. He had lost a great deal of weight. His hair and beard were long and matted with blood that oozed from the wounds inflicted by his captors. They would torture him every day for a week and then when he was near death, they would increase his rations, let him rest and recover – then start all over again.

One day around noon they unlocked his cell door and dragged him out near the beach. He could see very little in the bright sunlight. He tried to rub his eyes, but a soldier kicked him in the stomach so hard he doubled over and fell face down in the sand. He lay there for quite some time trying desperately to breathe. The officer came down from the cave, walked past Doug and then stopped. All the men just stood there silently staring at him, waiting for his next order. He turned around and looked at Doug lying on the sand. Finally, he reached into his pocket, and with a smile pulled out a handful of bamboo splints. Handing a few to one soldier, he shouted, "Yankee Dog! Where is your base? How many planes do you have there?" Doug said nothing. He again screamed at the men, "Make him talk!" They all grabbed Doug and held him down as one soldier bent his arm back and stepped on his wrist. He then twisted his hand until it nearly broke. Again the officer screamed, "Make him talk!" The soldier holding the bamboo splints took one and brutally shoved it under Doug's fingernail. He yelled as blood gushed out of his finger. "You bastard!" Doug yelled at him. The officer just smiled. "Put him in the tank!" he yelled. "A few days there and he will beg to talk." With that he started back to the cave. The men dragged Doug over to a clearing; then threw him feet first into what appeared to be a small barrel buried in the sand. A heavy iron door slammed shut, striking him so hard on the head it knocked him unconscious.

Hours later he opened his eyes, but again could see nothing but a few rays of sunlight burning down through the small slits in the iron door. His whole body was racked with pain. He found he could neither stand up nor sit down. There was room for him to stay in only one crouched position. The heat was now like a blast furnace. As the hours went by, the pain in his knees, back, and neck was unbearable. He kept saying over and over, "I'll kill you, you son-of-a-bitch! I'll kill you!" When night came, the only difference was

64

the heat subsided. But by now Doug was barely conscious.

The next day the sun again blazed down on the iron lid which sealed the small chamber Doug was entombed in. His hand had swollen to nearly twice its normal size. His arm and shoulder ached beyond endurance. His whole body was afire with pain. He desperately pushed again and again against the iron lid, but it was weighted down, making it impossible for him to move it. Later that day he again collapsed, and sagged motionless in the small pit.

It was nearly dark when two soldiers lifted the lid and pulled him out. They dragged him back to the cave and threw him into the cell. One soldier threw a bucket of water on him and then forced some down his throat, making him cough and choke. He tried to straighten his knees, but they were numb. The soldiers went out and locked the cell door.

The next morning he opened his eyes and saw some food and water on the floor close to the door. He dragged himself over to it and struggled through the process of trying to eat and drink.

It was two more days before he could stand up again. He slowly walked around his small cell. About then, a guard came in. He smiled and said something in Japanese as he sat some more food and water down. "Oh, Hell!" Doug said, "here we go again. More of your damn rest and rehabilitation program so you can torture me some more. Well, I got news for you. If I ever get the chance, I'll kill every one of you lousy bastards and buster, that's not a threat – it's a fact!"

Chapter Thirteen

Lowie had kept in close contact with Doug's family, but no further news had been released by the government. He was still missing in action. The war in Europe was now coming to a close and all the attention was shifting to the Japanese and bringing the Empire to its knees with an all-out effort to end the war in the Pacific. Every day she would listen to newscasts and check the papers for a ray of hope as a few prisoners were being rescued. But every day her hopes would be turned into more bitter disappointment. With her full-time job and several volunteer activities, her lifestyle was quite demanding. She felt it best to keep busy, allowing her less and less time to brood over what was to be – and now, may never be. Her days all ended the same way; in her room with the lights low, soft music coming from the radio. Her final thoughts of the day were all of Doug and her never-ending hope of his safe return. As the months slipped by, everyone's hopes were growing more dim, but she remained strong in her belief that the war would end and sometime – somehow – he would come home.

Chapter Fourteen

For some two weeks now, Doug's rations had been increased somewhat, with no torture, no beatings, and no interrogations. His mind had cleared and he felt much stronger again. Not knowing their motives, he tried to anticipate their next move. He was sure whatever it was, he would be the loser.

One day his guard opened the cell door and motioned him out. As he walked out into the sunlight, it was difficult to see. He shielded his eyes for quite some time. The guard shouted at him and by now, he recognized that as an order to "stop". After standing for what seemed a long time, the naval officer approached and ordered the guard to carry some boxes out of his quarters. He then told Doug everyone was needed to carry equipment down to a small boat. They were loading everything they could, including some personnel into the submarine lying just offshore. Everyone seemed excited. Doug was looking around trying to get a picture of this operation. He counted about twenty-five men and noticed a shack which was camouflaged. It appeared to be a radio center! That's what this place was – a radio outpost. But something was up. It looked like the island was a sinking ship and everyone was trying to get out. After two or three hours the officer shook hands with everyone; with some of the men bowing as he stepped into the boat. He took twenty men with him and they went out to the submarine. Everyone boarded and quickly the sub disappeared. That left only five soldiers. Two of them went over to the radio shack and the other three took Doug back into the cave. They locked him in the cell again – then returned to their quarters a little further back in the cave.

Early the next morning they led Doug outside. Using nearly perfect English, one soldier said, "Captain Stewart – I'm Sergeant Sueko and I'm now in charge here. Whether you live or die is my choice. We need a laborer here, so for now you live. I warn you, Yankee, the first time you cause me woe is when you die. There is no need to think of escape. This is a small island. It is very remote

– chosen for our purpose because it is out of all shipping lanes; and until we came, it was never inhabited. Your schedule is quite simple. To stay alive, you will do the work around here that we need done. You will eat what we give you. You understand?" Doug nodded yes. With that, Sueko led him back into the jungle some distance behind the radio shack where their fuel supply tank was hidden. He was instructed to carry fuel for the generator which took several trips a day. Thus started his many jobs which kept him working twelve to fourteen hours a day, seven days a week. The weeks passed and he now knew everything about the camp. Everything centered around the radio transmitter. Without it, they would be isolated from the rest of the world. They made quite sure he never got close to the radio equipment.

One night, shortly after they locked him in his cell, he heard a lot of yelling and everyone was running in and out of the cave. Carrying things, they were trying to secure everything, both inside and outside. He now could hear the wind starting to roar. Just then, Sueko ran by his cell. He asked what was happening. Sueko stopped just a few seconds, looked at him and then yelled, "Typhoon!" The next time Sueko came into the cave he was carrying a piece of the radio equipment. After stacking it on top of the other crates they had brought into the cave, he came over to Doug's cell. He unlocked the door. Sueko shouted, "We must bring all the radio equipment in here. Come with me!" As they started out of the cave, the wind hit with full fury, trees came crashing down – the wind and driving rain was devastating! It forced them back into the cave. Two of the other soldiers came running in. They were shouting and waving their arms in disgust. It was evident everyone would have to wait out the storm in the cave. Doug wondered what happened to the other two soldiers. The storm continued late into the night.

At first dawn, as quickly as it came, the storm was over. Everyone went outside to survey the damage and look for the other two men. The radio shack was completely destroyed. They found the two soldiers beneath the rubble with several trees and other debris piled on top. It was quite evident they were dead. Doug was ordered to dig graves for the two men. After placing the bodies and filling the graves, Sueko ordered him to clear the radio shack and place all the equipment on the remaining floor, which he did. The job required the rest of the day to complete. For the next week his three captors tried in vain to assemble and repair the radio. But the job became hopeless. Everyone knew they were now cut off from the rest of the world. All they could do was maintain living quarters and try to keep their food storage in order. There were ample supplies in the cave and plenty of fish available. Water was no problem.

Another month passed and still no vessels came to the rescue. The war was nearly over but they had no way of knowing that, or for that matter what was happening on the other islands in the area. It was obvious to Doug they were abandoned and the Japanese government was never coming back for them.

Many miles from this small outpost, a B-29 bomber was lifting off the runway, turning to a heading that would carry it over Japan. Only a few men in the whole world knew the war was to end very soon. Even more dramatically than it began. With the conclusion of this bombing mission, the world and all of its population would be altered forever. Few knew what atomic energy was and fewer still could comprehend the devastating power that was soon to be released on the planet Earth.

Chapter Fifteen

"Japan Surrenders – War's Over!" The newspapers across the country were all extolling the good news to everyone. Broadcasting companies had their radios blaring the great event and people were dancing in the streets from the largest cities to the smallest towns. The happy celebrations went on all through the night. For most, it was the happiest time of their lives, but for others such as Lowie, it was a bittersweet, empty feeling. She watched the happy, excited people, but now felt alone and sad. Her love was lost and the beautiful picture of her life was now a shattered loss. She turned and slowly walked back to her home. The night was clear and warm. As she walked alone she found herself searching for their star. It was not there.

In the weeks that followed, she kept a close vigil on all the news; both in the papers and on the radio. She found herself going to all the movies, searching the faces of the servicemen shown returning in the newsreels, hoping somehow he would be one of them. But each night she left the theater more lonely and depressed. Sometimes stopping at the drug store for a soda, she would sit for a long time and be unaware of the people around her. Her thoughts were all of her brief but happy life with the love she knew would be part of her life forever. Recalling every happy moment they spent together, her last thought was always of Doug with his arms around her, standing on the hill, looking out over the ocean, as he softly said, "I'll be back, honey. Someway, somehow, I'll be back. I promise." It was with that promise and all their memories made together that dominated her life as the months slipped by.

She had tried and succeeded in acquiring a job with the local telephone company. It was a job which she liked very much and her fellow employees were, for the most part, happy and friendly people. She became very close friends with two of the girls whose jobs were in the same field as her own. It was this basis that led to their early friendship, and as time passed, the three became quite close. A friendship she would, in the future, be grateful for, as it filled a part of the void in her life. The subject of boyfriends came up often, but it was a phase of life she was not prepared to undertake as yet. She just couldn't bring herself to meet any men, no matter how nice they may appear. Memories fade slowly if they are good memories. And for her, she had the best.

Chapter Sixteen

Doug was cleaning a pile of fish his captors had brought in from the bay. After what must have been nearly two years he was surprised they were still so secretive about their activities on the island. In all that time only four aircraft flew over their island and then they were so high no one could identify them. In the last year no one or nothing came near the island. He often wondered if the war was over. Three months earlier he had started to ask Sueko what his theory was on this. But one of the other soldiers hit him with his rifle butt, knocking him unconscious for a long time. Sueko was treating him better now, but the other two were brutal. He tried to stay away from them as much as he could. He was sure if he got the chance he would kill them both; but as yet, they held all the cards. The months passed and it was a dull, boring, and monotonous life the four of them were enduring.

When the main party left the island, they took all the clocks, calendars, cameras, binoculars, everything – leaving the soldiers who remained with nothing. It was as if they knew they would never be back. Doug was sure the war had turned against Japan and either this outfit was called home to fight an invasion or they were expecting our bombs to start dropping on them and they got out fast. There were still some bottles of sake in the cave and when they would decide to get drunk they first made sure Doug was handcuffed and locked in his cage. Sometimes they were drunk for two or three days. During those times, Doug kept very quiet, so as not to attract undue attention, fearing they might decide to use him for target practice. This was the type of life he was forced to live, year in and year out.

One morning Sueko unlocked Doug's cell and told him to get the fishing pole and come with him. They started down to the beach. When the other two soldiers saw them, they yelled something at Sueko which, of course, Doug didn't understand, but he knew it irritated Sueko. As he angrily snapped orders to them, they just stood where they were for a few moments and then quickly turned around and hurried back towards the cave. After he and Sueko were fishing for about an hour, Doug said, "Sergeant, what was that all about back there?"

Sueko looked at him for a long time and then he said, "Captain, my men want to kill you and then we three to do the honorable thing; commit hara-kiri. You see, you're still alive only because I outrank them. Because I was educated in the United States and they can't speak or understand English, they suspect you and me if I speak to you in English. They are getting paranoid about this. I don't know how long this can go on."

"Sueko, do you know how damn long it's been since your outfit left this island? And what's the story? Were they supposed to come back or what?"

"No, Captain, I don't know how long it's been. We were ordered to man the radio as long as we could and if our forces recaptured two of the important island groups we had lost, someone would relieve us. Of course, they purposely took all devices used to record time so we don't know how long a situation like this can endure. But I can tell by your beard we have been here quite a while." With that, he smiled. It was the first time Doug saw a smile in what he had guessed had been around three years.

"Let's face it," Doug said, "I think the damn war is over and I can't think that anyone knows we are on this lousy island."

"Captain, don't you ever say that to the other two. They are what you in America call fanatics. And if my superiors would hear me saying that, I would be shot for treason."

"So," Doug asked, "what do you think about the war? Do you think it's over?"

Sueko didn't answer. He just stood there, gazing out into space. Then, finally, nodded his head as if to say "yes". They stood there just looking at each other for some time and then Doug softly asked, "Who do you think won?"

"We had better get the fish back to camp," Sueko said, "and remember, this conversation never took place." Doug nodded, picked up the fish, and went back to the cave.

A few days later they had Doug gathering firewood from along the shore. Sueko came down from camp and relieved the guards, sending them back to the cave with wood. When the soldiers were out of sight, Doug asked Sueko where he went to school. "San Francisco," he answered.

"How would you like to get back there?"

Sueko looked around and then, when he was sure the other two men couldn't hear, he asked, "You have a plan?"

"My plane I flew in here. If I could repair it, I might be able to get it out and there's room enough for two in the cockpit if the cockpit was altered some. One problem is getting it down to the beach again. It would take some doing. Can you arrange it so I can go back to where it is and check out the damage? It was probably damaged by the storm, too."

"I'll think about it," Sueko answered. "Gather up that wood. We must get back to camp." The conversation ended and Doug filled the big sling he had made to carry firewood. They returned to the cave.

A few days later while Doug was doing some cleanup work, Sueko walked by and then stopped, came back and watched Doug for quite some time. "Tomorrow I'm sending my men on a reconnaissance mission to the other side of the island. There may be a better location for our camp. It will take them a couple of days. While they are gone, we will talk." He then walked away towards the beach. About an hour later, Doug was finished with his job. As he started back to the cave, he saw Sueko was still sitting on a rock near the water's edge. He was gazing out over the ocean.

Doug couldn't help but wonder what might be going through his mind. He was sure Sueko was very, very troubled.

The next day after his two men had left, Sueko unlocked the cell door as he said, "Let's look at that airplane of yours." They walked down the beach for quite some distance, then started back through the jungle. The plane was nearly two hundred yards away from the beach. Originally, they had cut all the trees down and pulled the plane back to hide it.

Doug walked up to it and as he stood there looking, he said, "Lady, you sure look good to me. I wish I had you in the air right now."

"Well, Captain," Sueko said, "check this thing out and see if it's possible, or are we on this island for life?"

Doug stared at the engine and made a complete walk-around inspection of the craft. Finally, he looked at Sueko. "Not bad," he said. "I think it can be repaired. There was very little storm damage to it. I'm really surprised. I'll open the engine cowlings first and really go over everything at the engines. If they can be repaired, I know the airframe can be patched up. When will your men be back?"

"Day after tomorrow," Sueko answered.

"That's not nearly time enough. Besides that, we have a lot of other problems such as filling the fuel tanks; also oil, and some way of propping the engines through to get them started. You know the batteries are no good. And another problem is getting this thing out to the beach. It's going to take all four of us somehow. After I get it ready we're going to have to trick them into helping with the move from here to the beach."

"But how?" Sueko asked. "How do you plan to do that?"

"I don't know yet, but I'll think of something. After all, we sure have plenty of time. I'll start with this engine – this is the one I lost oil pressure on. I remember, I shut it down right away; and then later the temperature started to climb on the other one. That's when I decided to bring the bird down and take my chances. So, several years later, here we still stand, looking at our only hope of ever getting off this godforsaken island. I say 'let's give it a shot'."

"I agree, Captain," Sueko said. "We will work together. You let me know what you need as your work progresses and I will try to smuggle it out here to the plane. We will have to be very careful about the whole project."

"Okay," Doug said, "I know we can use some of the things from the engine room of the dynamo, and they're far enough back of the camp that the other two won't notice when things are missing. Let's face it – they never go back there anyway. They don't have to as long as they have me for their slave and I know there's plenty of gas and oil. I ought to know. I carried enough of the damn stuff back from the storage tanks to the generator shack. So now, Sarge, you can do some carrying. This baby holds a lot of gas, and we want the tanks full. I'll start on the engines and you drain whatever is left in the tanks now, so we get all the condensation out. We want clean, dry tanks first – so let's go to work."

By the time the other two soldiers returned from their scouting trip of the island, Doug had already replaced some oil lines, on the one engine, that had been severed by some of the bullets that found their mark during the air battle. He had removed the spark plugs and rotated the props several times. Neither engine was seized tight. That was the first and most critical obstacle that faced them.

This meant that all the other problems could be overcome. When he went to sleep that night, he felt excited and very pleased with their progress so far.

Now with the other two back in camp it was nearly impossible for Doug to go near the plane. He made a list of things he would need when they resumed work again. Waiting for his opportunity, Doug gave the list to Sueko. Since he held the senior rank of the three, he was never questioned on his movements. It had been two weeks and Doug had no opportunity to get back to the plane. Sueko was working on a plan to get his two subordinates out of the area. One day he took Doug down to the beach to get some more fish. While they were there, he told Doug he had a plan. He had told the other two to start constructing a high tower which they could use as a lookout. That would enable them to keep a vigil for any ships that might come close to their island. Through his persistence, they agreed the idea had merit. They would also construct another tower to use as a fire signal. Doug immediately started drawing up plans for the construction; the plans he knew would take them months to complete. First it would take a thorough survey of the island to find the best spot for the project. Then, to amass all the lumber and equipment needed, would take weeks of hard work. This would give him a lot of time to work on the plane. He explained all of this to Sueko, reminding him, they must have the job done before the lookout tower was high enough to spot the work being done on the aircraft. It would be up to Sueko to convince his partners to do the job themselves, out of fear that if they used their prisoner to do the work, he might try to sabotage the whole project.

A few days later, Sueko had the fist phase of the big job under-way. His two men had picked supplies and started out on a reconnaissance expedition to find the right spot for construction. This left Doug and Sueko with lots of time to do their work on the plane.

For the next several weeks, Doug worked on the aircraft every day. Sueko divided his time between that work and his men. And both projects progressed surprisingly well.

One day, Sueko came back to where Doug was working on the plane. He smiled and asked, "Can we fly yet?"

"Sarge," Doug said, as he wiped some grease from his hands, "if we had it on the beach and some way to spin the props, she would fly away."

They shook hands and then both broke into laughter. It was clear Sueko was as happy as Doug with the thought of getting off this island. That night Doug was sitting at the entrance of the cave resting. He could do this some nights as the other two soldiers would stay at the construction site two or three days at a time. As usual, his thoughts drifted back to Lowie and the folks back home, and he wondered if everyone had given up on his returning. He was sure they had, as he guessed it must have been three to four years now since he landed on this island – and the chances of someone missing in action, returning after that much time, were highly unlikely.

"What a strange twist of fate," he said out loud.

"What did you say?" Sueko asked.

"Oh, I was just thinking out loud, Sarge; thinking about my folks back home and my girlfriend I left behind. I wonder if she gave up on me and married someone else by now. She was everything I ever wanted; so beautiful, kind and gentle…" he said, as his voice trailed off to a whisper. "Everything," he repeated. "Everything."

"You love this girl?" Sueko asked.

"More than anything in this world," Doug answered. They sat in silence for a long time. Doug finally asked, "Do you have a wife or girlfriend?"

"No," Sueko answered. "Not yet – maybe someday."

It was now getting late and Sueko said, "Okay, Captain, in the cell again; just in case they come back." Doug got up and took one last look for the star he had promised Lowie. Again, it was not there. He went into the cell and lay on his cot for a long time, thinking of those wonderful times with her. The depression was overwhelming and as he drifted off to sleep, tears ran down his cheeks.

For the next several weeks, Doug spent what spare time he had trying to devise a system to substitute the starting system of the plane's engines. The batteries were of no use since they had not been charged for several years. He had to make a small model of an engine and propeller and with that he tried different methods of spinning the prop fast enough to ignite the engine. After several nights of failures, he finally met with some success. When he had most of the flaws worked out of it, he showed it to Sueko. He was impressed and thought it had a good chance of success. They would need two long pieces of rope and a bamboo hoop large enough to fit over the three-bladed propellers of the plane. After wrapping the rope around the outside edge of the loop, they would need some method of power to pull the rope which, in turn, would unwind; thereby spinning the props fast enough to start the engines. The last big hurdle was what to use for the power.

Doug pondered the problem for several days and finally decided to try using the coconut trees around the plane. He explained to Sueko he would need a chain hoist and some more rope. They would select a tree that was best in alignment with the propeller, fasten the hoist to the top of the tree and try to bend it down as much as possible; then secure it in that position and fasten the rope that was wrapped around the hoop on the prop. When all was ready, Sueko would use an ax and cut the restraining line, allowing the tree to snap back up. He told Sueko it sounded like one of "Rube Goldberg's" brainstorms, but it might just work. If not at first, they had nothing but time to try again and again; or, make whatever modifications would improve the mechanism. Sueko just smiled and then said, "First, I'll get the chain hoist. I know we have some in crates at the back of the generator shack."

There was no work done either on the plane or on the tower for the next four days, as the weather turned bad. This meant all four men stayed in the cave; Doug in his cell and his captors in their quarters. He used the time for more planning on his next project; but the lull in activity allowed sadness to set in again. With all his thoughts of what might have been, the only life and love he ever wanted; and as the years passed, it was slipping further and further away from him, he had to be realistic. No love, even such as the love he had back home could survive all these years without some thread of real hope; and that thread had been severed a long time ago. He just sat in his cell and stared into space for a long time, but he just couldn't make his heart believe it was all over.

The next day, the storm passed and the two men went back to their job on the lookout tower. Doug and Sueko sat down to talk over the next few steps of their project. They both knew even if the plan to start the engines did work, they would make so much noise the other men would hear them.

Doug convinced Sueko to start talking to his men about making their presence on the island as visible as possible now. And one way would be to move the airplane out of the jungle and onto the beach. He could tell them he would make the Yankee do whatever was necessary to get the plane down to the beach and park it where it could be seen from above, as well as from any ship that might pass close enough. Sueko's big job would be convincing his men this would be the best thing to do at this time. The next day, Sueko called his men over to the cave for a meeting. They talked for a long time and finally they shook hands, bowed to each other, and the two went back to the lookout tower they were building. Sueko hurried over to where Doug was cleaning some fish. He smiled and said, "Okay, Captain, it's your show from here on. Let's try to get that thing of yours started."

"Will do, Sarge; but you keep those fellows of yours well informed and off my back. I'm allergic to having my head chopped off."

"No problem, Captain. They now think it's a great idea. But they don't think it can be done."

"Well, we don't have anything else to try so what's to lose?" Doug said.

With that settled, they both hurried back to the plane. After everything was ready, Doug again removed the spark plugs which would allow the engine to rotate much easier. Now they are ready for their first test. When Doug gave the signal, Sueko chopped the restraining rope, allowing the tree to swing back upright, pulling the engine rope in doing so. As it did, the engine rotated nearly six times quite easily. "It will work," Doug shouted. "I'll put the plugs back in the cylinders and tomorrow morning this baby is going to come alive again! Look out – 'Wild Blue Yonder' – here we come!"

Chapter Seventeen

It was early in the morning when Doug and Sueko started winding the rope around the engine prop again. "This time it's for real," Doug said. "I'll prime the engine and when I flip the switch, you cut the rope and stand back. If it starts, I'll let it run very slowly and hope this hoop contraption comes apart without damaging the side of the fuselage. Then you go around to the other engine. When I signal, cut that rope. If all goes well, I'll let them run as long as the fuel in the tanks lasts. Just hope the batteries will still take a charge. If they do, we'll really have it made."

After several hours of preparation, everything was ready. Doug climbed into the cockpit, checked and double-checked everything, this time it was for real. When he was sure everything was ready, he signaled Sueko, who was poised with the ax in position. With full force, the ax severed the rope, allowing the tall tree to snap violently upright. The prop was spinning! After several popping explosions, smoke poured out the exhaust stacks. An instant later, the big engine came alive with a loud roar. Doug looked down from the cockpit with a big smile. He gave Sueko the "thumbs-up" sign. Sueko was laughing; jumping up and down, holding the ax high in the air. When the bamboo hoop on the prop came apart, the engine ran smoothly, with very little smoke coming from the exhaust port. Doug eased the throttle in to a fast-idle position. Everything was perfect; oil pressure was good, the generator was charging, everything on the instrument panel was indicating just what it should. He took a deep breath then signaled Sueko to release the other engine. He quickly ran over to the other side, raised the ax, and when Doug nodded his head, the ax came down. A few seconds later, this engine responded the same way. Now, with both engines roaring, Doug yelled at the top of his voice; giving Sueko the "thumbs-up" sign again. This was his baby and he was proud of her. He would keep the engines running as long as it would take to charge the batteries. He settled back in the seat for what would amount to nearly two hours of running time. When the charge-indicating gauges returned to the "zero" position, Doug was satisfied the batteries were fully charged and proceeded to shut the engines down. He climbed down from the cockpit, smiling. Sueko shook his hand and said, "Well Captain, your plane is ready to fly; are you?"

"The sooner the better, Sueko – the sooner the better! I'll check the craft out for leaks and then see if the batteries will do their job."

About half-an-hour later, he got his answer. When everything was ready he flipped the switches and the props started to spin. Within seconds, both engines were again roaring. He let them run for another hour and then shut them down again; well satisfied the plane was ready to fly.

The next day Doug and Sueko started clearing a path down to the beach. They worked for nearly a week. Some holes had to be filled; and all loose stones raked off. They removed everything that might be picked up by the props, causing damage. When all preparations were finished, the day finally arrived. Doug climbed aboard, fired up the engines, and started taxiing slowly down to the beach, being very careful every foot of the way. It was still a very rough, though short, trip. Finally his P-38 was once again sitting on the beach. He locked the brakes, eased the throttle in to a near maximum RPM setting. With both engines responding with a loud, singing roar, the whole craft shook. A moment later Doug throttled back, returning the engines to a smooth idle and then he shut them down. Climbing out of the cockpit, Doug stood on the wing, raised his arms high in the air, and shouted to Sueko, "WE DID IT! The big bird is ready to fly!"

"Not so loud, Captain. My men will hear you all the way up at the tower. Remember, they agreed to let us get it out here on the beach to help someone spot it and thereby arrange for our rescue from this island. That's all they agreed to. The plan you and I have is something else. So be careful from here on out."

The next morning Sueko and his two men were standing down on the beach at the plane. He was explaining how he and the Yankee managed to get the craft out of the jungle and down there. It was positioned at the best location for someone in the area to spot and maybe come in to investigate. He told them the plane was in no way able to fly. They argued a while on this point and finally Sueko ordered them back to the tower they were building. It must be completed as soon as possible. They became furious and wanted to shoot holes in the tires to make sure the prisoner did not escape in the plane. They insisted he send the Yankee with them to help on the tower project. Sueko had little choice but to agree. He knew they were very suspicious of him and Doug spending so much time together. He knew they were sure Doug and he were planning to escape and they would have to be very careful with the timing of the attempt. The two soldiers left Sueko and went up to the cave to get Doug. All the way over to the tower construction site, they complained bitterly to each other and it appeared to Doug they were scheming something; but not understanding Japanese, he had no idea what to expect. What he didn't know was that the two captors were going to kill him at the tower; but not shoot him (so as not to alert Sueko) and then destroy the plane. The one standing behind Doug quickly picked up a short piece of lumber and brought it crashing down on Doug's head. Everything went black and he fell face down in the sand. As the other used his foot to roll him over, blood was coming out of Doug's ears and mouth. After checking the body closer, they were satisfied he was, in fact, quite dead. They picked up their rifles and ran back to the plane. Sueko had just started to pour gas into the left tank when they arrived. Screaming in wild anger, they raised their rifles and started firing at him. He pulled his revolver and returned fire, hitting one soldier in the head. He staggered backwards and fell dead. The other soldier kept firing, with several bullets finding their mark. Sueko doubled over, then fell to the ground. A few moments later he was dead. The soldier looked around with terror-stricken eyes; then turned and ran back to the cave, gathering up some material which he then fashioned into a torch. He then got a ceremonial robe and went back down to the plane. After firing holes into the gas tanks, he lit the torch and hurled it at the gas streaming out of the plane. It instantly exploded into a roaring inferno. He backed away from the intense heat; then put the robe on, sat down on the sand, placed the rifle barrel in his mouth and with his feet, pressed the trigger. There was a sickening, awful explosion; and then there was total silence, except for the roaring fire, consuming the plane. Black smoke billowed, high out over the ocean.

When the sun rose the next day, the little island had returned to the stark silence it had kept for centuries past.

Chapter Eighteen

After thirty years of service with the Air Force, Colonel Meese, Lowie's father, had retired. Several years later he decided to start a travel agency. As the business increased it became apparent he would need help to satisfy the workload demands. After many discussions, he finally persuaded his daughter to come into the business, as a full-time partner. It was a whole new experience for her and, at first, she was not sure it was a good move on her part. However, the experience offered the confidence she needed and as time went by, she was quite happy she had made the job change. She became so immersed in the job that the first year slipped by very quickly. She now had her own apartment, was part-owner of a successful business, and for all practical purposes, was quite happy with life, but of course, she still had the one void that, from time to time, troubled her deeply. This being true, still only her very dear and closest friends knew this to be part of her life.

It was nearly five in the afternoon when two of Lowie's friends came into her office. "Hi Lowie, it's time to quit," the one said, "we're going to the base to play bingo. Why don't you come along? We really would like you to meet the fellow we've been telling you about." They had asked her many times through the years to join them, but Lowie always declined. They had met a Sergeant at the game, who, like Lowie, had lost a loved one, his wife of many years. He too had settled into a life devoted to his career in the Army, and raising a daughter who was now six years old. He never seemed interested in a social life, though he was handsome, well educated, and very pleasant to everyone. They just knew their two friends had to meet!

This time Lowie finally agreed to go along with them to the base. "Okay," she said, "I'll go with you, but don't get any ideas. I'll meet your friend and I promise I won't embarrass you."

They arrived early and decided to have a drink, before the game started. They were sitting at the table, and just as their drinks were being served, their friend came over. Lowie's two friends quickly started the introductions.

"Lowie, this is our good friend, Sgt. Thomas Brighton, Thomas, this is our dearest and most reluctant friend we have been telling you about, Lowie Meese."

The Sergeant smiled, "Hello Lowie, it is true I have heard a lot about you, and I must say, everything I have heard was very good, and from what I can see, is very true. I'm happy to meet such a beautiful lady."

When the game began, the four sat at the same table to play. There was a lot of laughing, and most of it was at Lowie's expense. This was her first attempt at playing bingo, and Thomas was more than willing to be her coach. It was quite obvious he was very attracted to the beautiful and charming lady he had just met.

When the evening ended, Thomas asked Lowie if she would join them next week. She smiled, "Yes I'll try it again. But can you help me win at least one game?"

He smiled, "If I have to I'll rig the game." He walked with them to their car, and thanked them for a wonderful evening, "Then I'll see you all next week?"

"Oh yes!" Lowie's friends answered quickly.

"Okay! Good night and drive safely," the Sergeant said as he walked away.

Each week their same persuasive manner brought the same results – a night of bingo at the base, and each night, Thomas would join them.

After several weeks, her friends brought their husbands along with them. This, in turn, became a small party for a few drinks and snacks after the game, of course, the Sergeant was invited along and so a friendship was born. This friendship was to take a strange twist later on.

After many weeks and a lot of requests, Lowie finally agreed to go out to a movie with the Sergeant. She put everything up front right away. They were now friends, and that's all it would ever be; just friendship. Period. He had been married. His wife had been killed in a car accident. He has a child; a girl six years old. He lived with his ailing mother just a few blocks from the Army Base. He was making a career of the Army and to this point, that was about the sum total of his life.

They started spending time together on Sunday afternoons. Most often, they took the little girl along when they went to a movie or just for a drive through the countryside. The three became very close. They would go shopping together, to a football game, or just stay home. For Robin, it didn't matter where they went or what they did, she had fun as long as she was with Lowie.

One evening, Thomas wanted to take a walk through the park. As he and Lowie were walking along, talking about Robin and how fast she was growing up, he stopped at a bench and asked her to sit down. He had something he wanted to talk about. They sat a few moments in silence and finally he asked her to marry him. "Before you answer, I know I was never to ask that question; but I've known you for nearly a year now, and you must know I love you."

She closed her eyes and softly said, "Please, Thomas, I can't marry you. I can't marry anyone. You don't know anything about my past. It may be hard for other people to understand, but you see, I was in love with an Air Force pilot. Before he went overseas, we both made a promise to wait. We were so in love, the time we had to wait meant nothing. Our whole life was in front of us. Just before he was about to be shipped back to the United States, his plane went down and no one has seen him since. That was many, many years ago and Thomas, I still can't let go. I just can't let go. I'm sorry. I'm truly sorry, but I can't."

With that, she burst into tears. Thomas put his arm around her. "I'm sorry, Lowie, I didn't know."

As she started to dry her eyes, she said, "It's okay, Thomas, you had no way of knowing. I do like you and I adore your little girl. But now I must remain as I am."

"What was his name?" he asked.

"Douglas Stewart," she answered, feeling proud to say his name. "He flew P-38s and went down in the South Pacific, but you would have to know him to believe that he would come back, and I never gave up that hope, even to this day, at times, I feel he will!"

"For your sake, Lowie, I truly hope he does."

The sun was just starting to sink below the horizon and the white clouds, scattered across the sky, quickly turned to bright gold. They got up from the bench and started walking slowly back home. As they walked along he put his arms around her, but neither said anything for a long time. As they approached Thomas's home, Robin saw them and came running to meet them.

One evening Thomas came to her apartment, and he was very

upset. He had just received his shipping orders for Vietnam and he wanted to talk to Lowie about his daughter Robin. While he would be gone, of course she would remain with her grandmother; but in the event something were to happen either to himself or Robin's grandmother, would Lowie help take care of Robin until she got through school, even by adoption if necessary? They talked for several hours and Lowie assured him she would do whatever was best for Robin. She and Robin were as close as mother and daughter now, so for as long as he was gone, there was no need to worry. She would always be properly cared for. They agreed to meet the next day at his mother's house and discuss it in full detail with Robin and Thomas's mother. The following evening, after several more hours of discussion, everyone was very much in favor of the arrangement. They were all sure they would work out any problems, no matter what might happen. But, of course, nothing was going to happen.

The following week, Thomas shipped out for Vietnam and set in motion a chain of events that would alter Lowie's life for many years to come. Robin spent most of the weekends with Lowie. It seems they had many things to do and lots of places to go. As the months wore on, they both looked forward to the times they spent together. Robin was doing quite well in school, as well as at home. She was always a very happy young lady and a delight to be with. They always reserved a portion of Sunday for the long letter to her dad. She would always assure him that everything back home was wonderful and as soon as he got back, it would be perfect.

It had been nearly a year now since he arrived in Vietnam and it was obvious by his letters, it was anything but good for him. It was clear from the news reports that both sides were suffering heavy casualties with no end in sight. Less than three weeks later his mother received the tragic news; her son was killed in action. The news was devastating to everyone, but for a young girl who had already lost her mother, it was an absolute tragedy. Lowie spent as much time as possible with her, though she knew comfort is both impossible to give or receive at a time like this.

With the coming weeks, the failing health of Robin's grandmother seemed to accelerate. This being quite evident, she called both her lawyer and Lowie to her home. She had her lawyer prepare the necessary papers for the adoption. After a full explanation of what would have to be done when the time came, the lawyer left the two and they completed all the remaining plans. Later that day, the old lady asked Lowie to assist her outdoors. She desperately wanted to go for a walk to the outer boundaries of her property, to the shore of the small lake. With great effort, they made it to the old park-style bench. The autumn leaves were beginning to fall and the wind swirled them around the old stone wall, which at places, had fallen down. It was indeed a picture of autumn in the east. The old lady held onto Lowie's hand as they sat and talked. "My dear young lady," she said, "you've been a real joy and comfort to all of us. I'm ever so grateful to have known you, if only for so short a time." There were tears in her eyes as she looked over the windswept lake. "My dear husband and I spent most of our lives here," she said. "Though he's been gone many years, sitting here now, I can still hear his warming laughter. He just loved it here, especially this time of the year. He always said October was the best month of the year and he decided to be born in this month to make it even better. He always liked to tease me. We spent many wonderful years right here by our lake. Years I'd give everything I have to live again with him. If just for a little while. They say old people just sit around and wait to die. My dear, if you have ever had a true love, no matter how old, you never want to let it go. The last words my dear man said, as he squeezed my hand with tears in his eyes, was 'my love – I don't want to go without you – I'm scared'. A moment later, he was gone. With him went my love. Of course, my life went on, but there was never again that love. My dear, do you know what I'm talking about, or do you just think I'm a babbling old fool?"

"I know exactly what you mean," Lowie answered. "You see, I had such a love. It was a long time ago. We were just two young kids. He was a pilot in the war and didn't make it back."

"I'm so sorry for him and you, my dear," the old lady said. "That war left so many scars on the young, such as you. We all hoped it would end wars and here we are again in still another." They both sat in silence for a long time. The heavy gray-blue sky let little sunlight through. The wind was getting cooler and finally the old lady asked Lowie to help her return to the house. The walk up the hill was quite difficult for her. About halfway up, she stopped, turned and took one final look. Just then the sun broke through and lit up the whole area. The leaves reflected a thousand shades of autumn and the cold dark lake below it was a picture only nature could produce. It was as if she knew this was the final view of her loving memories. Tears filled her eyes again and she slowly turned and whispered, "Thank you, my dear. Thank you for everything. I know my time is over and like my dear husband; I don't want to let go."

A lady and a young girl were the last to leave the gravesite on this cold, damp day. They stopped at the old iron gate, turned and looked back at the new grave. The lady paused, looking up at the cold, gray sky. She softly said, "Come on, dear, I'll take you home." She put her arms around the young girl and as they slowly walked away she said, "From now on Robin, it's you and me against the world." The little girl had just lost her last-known relative and what was once a happy and loving family was now reduced to a memory.

"What's going to become of me, Lowie?" Robin asked.

"From this moment on, dear, you're my daughter whom I love very much and I promise to be by your side, for as long as you need me. I'll need you for the rest of my life. What would I do without you?"

The weeks that followed were spent filling out all the necessary forms and legal actions to complete the adoption of Robin. The procedures were not without frustrations, but at last it was complete and now they were mother and daughter. It took several months for the lawyer to sell off the estate of Robin's grandmother, but at last everything was settled, with all proceeds going to a trust fund for Robin. The future would hold few financial worries for the little girl, but the heartbreaking loss for her would fade, oh, so slowly. But Lowie would help her pick up the pieces of her life and go on from there. As time passed, they took whatever free time they had for short trips, either shopping or just sightseeing. As they both liked to travel, these trips became more frequent and of longer durations. It had developed into a close and happy life for both.

One Saturday morning, Lowie returned from the grocery store to find Robin sitting on the bedroom floor, a small velvet-covered box in front of her. She was holding a pair of silver wings. "Hi, Mom," she called out. "I was cleaning the closet and found this box of pictures and things. Where did these come from?" she asked as she held up the wings. Lowie sat down at her side. Robin handed her the silver wings. She held them in her open hand a moment; then closed her hand and tears came to her eyes. "I'm sorry, Mother. What did I do?"

As she dried her eyes, she opened her hand and again looked at the small wings. "Memories, Robin, just memories. A young fellow gave me these on the day he graduated from flight school. His name was Doug Stewart and we were in love. We were to be married when he returned from overseas."

"What happened?" Robin asked.

"He never made it back. His plane went down in the South Pacific. They notified his parents. He was listed as missing-in-action, and presumed dead."

"You don't believe them, do you?"

"No, Robin, I don't. I know it's been many years now, but I still can't believe it. You see, dear, true love can give some of us a glimpse of real life, even though it's but a fleeting moment in our lifetime, we can never let go. It's that beautiful. And I've had that moment."

"Do you think you'll ever marry?" Robin asked.

"I don't know, dear. I really don't know. I guess whatever will be, will be."

"I was hoping you and my dad would get married, he really did love you."

"I guess he did, but Robin, the timing was all wrong. Maybe someday we would have, but with him going to a combat zone, I don't think I could go through that wait again; never knowing from day to day what to expect. It's a very sad and lonely life and the waiting is frightening. I really did care for your father, but I wouldn't allow myself to fall in love again."

"Do you have any pictures of Doug?" Robin asked.

"Just one snapshot he sent me from wherever he was in the Pacific. He was standing by his plane and one of his buddies snapped it. They had just painted my name on the side of his aircraft. The guys all did that then. They'd name their planes in honor of their moms, or wives, or girlfriends. Some just painted crazy names on them." She got up and went over to the dresser, opened the drawer and took the picture out, handing it to Robin.

"Wow, Mom, he's terrific! He looks like a movie star."

"I thought so, but he had a lot more than good looks. He was the kind of a fellow all girls want to meet sometime in their life, but deep down, know they won't. I did, though for just a brief time, but I wouldn't trade those moments for anything in the world. I just hope you meet that kind of a young man someday; but of course, not for a few years yet." They both laughed as she placed the picture back in the drawer. "Now put the wings back in the box and let's go get something to eat. I'm starved!"

As the months slipped by, Robin became more and more interested in her mother's travel agency. She spent a lot of time at the office after school. She was learning as much as possible about planning and coordinating trips all over the world. Lowie assured her if everything continued to go well with the business, the following year she would take her along on some of the tours. Lowie's father had been encouraging her to start heading some of the tours herself. It was a great opportunity to see the world and it would be a tremendous learning experience for Robin, on her summer vacations from school. There was an Australian trip coming, in about a year, and they both were excited as they started planning the basic groundwork for that tour. For Lowie it was an opportunity to see a part of the world Doug had been sent to, back during the war. Of course, everything was different now, but she still couldn't help thinking she might see some of the places he may have been. Remote as it might be, the thought was exciting and she was really looking forward to going. It would be the first tour she would be in charge of and that made her a little nervous.

Robin's summer vacation quickly passed and again she was back in school. With her studies and school activities, her life was quite active, causing the winter months to slip by. As spring was approaching again, she and Lowie both became more anxious for the arrival of July when the tour was to get underway. The itinerary was a flight from Harrisburg International with an eventual destination being Sydney, Australia. From there, the tour would start a return by sea, with a host of port calls along the way and finally returning by way of the canal to Philadelphia. All in all, it would be an eight-week tour. Although the cost was substantial, all reservations were sold in a matter of two to three months from the announcement date. For Lowie and her father, this tour would be a real financial success. For Robin as well as her mother, it would be the thrill of a lifetime. After all the planning and requirements were met, the group was off on the first leg of a long, and hopefully happy, journey. San Francisco would be on the first stop and that would be of short duration, and then out over the Pacific. Next stop – Hawaii for a few days, and then on to Sydney. There the group would spend a full week taking side trips by both train and bus.

The time passed quickly, and before anyone was ready, it was time to board the luxury liner – and on with the tour. Next stop – Wellington, New Zealand. That was a planned five-day stop with lots of free time for everyone. Of course, with each stop-off, there were different types of problems for Lowie. But with each, she acquired more experience and her job became more enjoyable. As she told Robin at this point, she wouldn't trade her job for any in the world. A few days later and it was off to Port Moresby, New Guinea. That would be another five-day stop, with a lot of island hopping. All along the trip they had gotten more than their share of good weather and when a rainy day came along, everyone stayed aboard ship to indulge in good food and lots of relaxation. At the end of this day, it was up with the anchor and on with the tour.

On the first night out of port, the ship's cruise director planned a nostalgia night for lovers, with the big-band sound. The dance floor was crowded when the band played several Glenn Miller hits from World War II. Robin went out at the insistence of Lowie to dance with a young boy in the tour. The female vocalist picked up the mike and started to sing "Oh, Give Me Something to Remember You By." When Robin came back to the table, Lowie was gone. She asked where her mother was. Someone in their group said she went out on deck, she said she would be back in a few minutes. Robin went out looking for her. The moon was so bright, it was reflecting on the water. She saw her mother standing by the rail. As she walked over, she asked, "Are you all right, Mother?"

"Yes, dear, I guess the song got to me. As they say, that was 'our song' and when I heard it, the years melted away, and Doug was with me again for a few minutes." She leaned against the rail and was looking out over the ocean. Robin put her arm around her and they stood there in silence for quite a while. Then Lowie softly said, "I guess this is why I wanted to take this tour so badly. You see, he went down somewhere in this part of the world, and I know my coming here in no way solves the mystery of his disappearance, but deep down, I still always wanted to come over here just to see, and be near the area where he went down and I'm really glad I got the opportunity. Just standing here, looking out over this area, I feel very close to him and it's a warm feeling I'll never forget. I think I needed this and by the time we get back home again, I may be able to go on with my life a lot easier. It's something that tormented me for years and years; but now, I think I can lay it aside." She unfastened a small corsage Robin had given her earlier. She held it in her hand a long time, then tossed it into the sea. "Goodbye, dear heart, I loved you so much. May God be with you wherever you are…" and her voice trailed off. "I love you." As Robin stood holding onto her arm, she started to cry. "Don't cry, dear, everything must come to an end. Some things sooner than others – that's all – but we must always go on. Come on, dear, let's go back to the party."

There were many port calls on the way back to the Panama Canal. Once there, the ship anchored for the final port call. They spent one day and night at the Canal Zone. Then it was on to Philadelphia. From there, Robin and Lowie took a commercial flight to Harrisburg. Lowie's parents were waiting for them and after all the luggage was picked up, they returned to a little "welcome home" party. A few friends had stopped by and everyone was asking questions about the trip. It was quite late when they got back to their own apartment.

They took the next day off for unpacking and getting re-established in their home life routine. Then it was back to work for Lowie. She and her father had planned two more cruises; one to the Caribbean and one to the Azores. Business could not be better. She was kept so busy she couldn't believe the summer was over and Robin was back in school again.

The next year she and Robin organized another trip. This one was to the British Isles. It was a small group from the local area and a few of the people Lowie knew, because she had been to school in the area. Renewing old acquaintances made it a fun trip. As the trip progressed, she met an old classmate who had been divorced for several years. He decided on the trip after his doctor advised him to take a vacation from the business world he was involved in. His name was Bill Jacoby. It had been years since they had last seen each other. They had dinner together the first night out. They spent the entire evening together, talking over old times. Lowie made it clear during their conversation that there are certain rules tour directors must abide by. The most important one is no involvement with clients. Bill understood and agreed that theirs would be a very casual friendship.

It was nearly a month after the cruise before Bill called and asked her to have lunch. As the months passed, they spent more and more time together; but they were both in agreement, marriage was not the goal. So with this friendship, the next few years slipped by and they spent as much time together as possible. Because of their business life that time was sparingly available.

Chapter Nineteen

Weeks earlier, unknown to Lowie and Robin, the sun rose on a bright clear day far away in another part of the world. The captain of a small oil-exploration ship was getting a report from his maintenance chief. They just had a complete power failure and it would take at least twenty-four hours to repair. He asked for and received an exact fix on their location. Checking this with his charts, he found they were more than two hundred and fifty miles from New Guinea. There were many small islands around them. The closest was one with no inhabitants and very small; off to their starboard side. He calculated the distance as 2.3 miles. Since their repairs would not be completed for twenty-four hours, he called a few crew members and told them to prepare their launch for a trip ashore. With their ship at anchor, and the weather reports very good, they might as well check out the area. An hour later everything was ready. Among their equipment the Captain had ordered firearms, binoculars and small transceiver radio equipment. He told the radioman to stand by. They would keep in contact just in case any trouble developed. The four men climbed aboard the small boat, started the engine and headed for the little island. After traveling to within a few hundred yards of the beach, the Captain who had been checking the area with his binoculars, dropped his hand to his side, still holding the glasses. He had a puzzled look on his face as if not believing what he saw. Again he raised the binoculars. He started to point off to their left. "Over there," he called. "Steer towards that area. I think I see some wreckage of some kind. It's beyond the beach area. Back at the tree line."

"What is it Captain?" one man asked.

"I don't know, but it looks like metal pieces of something. Maybe a boat broken up. Aside from that, the island looks pretty dead. In fact, it's a little scary. Of the thousands of inhabited islands in this part of the world, it seems no two are alike, and you never know what to expect if you go ashore. Cut the engine, we'll drift in from here," he ordered. As the boat ran aground, everyone jumped out and hurried over to the wreckage.

"What do you think it is, Captain?" As they came closer it was obvious it was the remains of an airplane. The Captain told his men to spread out and look for skeletons or anything that might help identify the wreckage. He started pulling back some of the charred metal strips and under one of the bent flaps he quickly rubbed at a small metal tag. It was obvious the craft had burned. There was a lot of meltdown on the aluminum and he rubbed the small plate and found what he was looking for. Near the partly destroyed wing spar was a manufacturer's tag. With his handkerchief he rubbed some of the oxidation from it and read "Lockheed Corp., Burbank, California." "It's one of ours," he called out to his men. They all came running back to the craft. "It's a Lockheed and from the size of it, I'd guess it's a P-38 fighter. You men find anything?"

"Nothing, Captain. What do you think happened?"

He stood and looked at the wreckage a while and then said, "I don't think it crashed in the ocean and washed up on the beach. There does not seem to be much salt-water damage. I'd guess it landed here, then caught fire and burned. Through the years, storms probably pushed it back here among the trees."

"Wonder what happened to the pilot?" one man asked.

"I'll make contact with our ship and let them know what we found."

"This will take some time. We'll check the whole area out. No telling what we might find." After making several attempts, he finally received a response from his radioman on board. He explained everything up to that point and told the crew they would return to the ship by sundown. He would check in with them from time to time. He asked the radioman to keep a close eye on the conditions in the area. Also, give him updates on the repair work aboard ship. He told them they were ready to start exploring the island. The Captain told the men to stay close and stay in contact with each other. He explained they would make their way inland for one-half-hour; then make a $90°$ turn to the right; stay on that heading for just ten minutes; and then again make a $90°$ turn to the right, which would eventually bring them back on the beach. Another right turn staying on the beach would bring them back to their boat. After checking their watches, they started inland, moving very slowly and carefully. About ten minutes later, one of the men held up his hand signaling the captain to come over to where he was standing. The Captain made his way to where the crewman was. He pointed to something directly in front of him. Some two hundred yards away there appeared to be a cave entrance. The Captain raised his binoculars and for several minutes studied the whole area in front of them. Without speaking, he nodded his head in agreement.

"Is it a cave?" one man whispered.

Again he lowered his binoculars. Looking at his men, he whispered, "It sure is; and not just a cave, but there is some equipment around the entrance. Someone has been living on this island. We can't know if they are friendly or not, so we're not taking any chances. We'll go back to the ship and when the repairs are finished, we can move in a little closer. Then come back with more men and equipment and find out just what the story is here." They returned to the beach, found their boat and very quietly started back out to the ship.

When they came aboard, everyone was curious as to what they found on the island. The Captain called everyone up on deck and after explaining what they saw, he asked for a few volunteers to go back the next day, to see if anyone was still using the cave. As it turned out, nearly everyone wanted to go. This left the captain with no choice but to pick nine men to go with him.

By noon the next day, the repairs on the ship were completed and they had moved in closer to the island. They dropped anchor less than half a mile out from the beach. After loading two boats with supplies and weapons, they started in to the beach. Once on shore, they hid the boats and each man took his weapons and supplies as quietly as possible. They formed two parties, about fifty yards apart, and started towards the cave. When less than a hundred yards from the entrance, the Captain signaled for everyone to stop. He again studied the cave entrance with his binoculars. After several minutes he turned to his men and in a hushed voice said, "There's no doubt about it, this island has had some inhabitants, or still does."

"Can you see anything moving?" someone asked.

"No. How about you other men?"

"No, Captain," each one answered. "Just some old crates and boxes, or what's left of them."

"Well, we're not moving in any closer until I'm sure no one is home. We'll just wait here for a while. We'll sit this out about an hour. If nothing happens, we'll go in." They all nodded in agreement.

The Captain turned his radio on and, in a quiet voice, called out to the ship. After several attempts, he got a response. The radioman sounded concerned as he asked if they had found anything and if everything was okay. He assured the men on board, he and his crew were in no danger. Things were very quiet and unless something changed, they were going into the cave to have a look. In any event he would keep them informed. If they needed help, he would yell for them loud and clear. With that, he signaled off and slipped the button off on the radio.

About an hour later, the captain whispered, "Okay, let's go! Now be careful. Don't do anything stupid." Cautiously, they worked their way towards the cave entrance. The Captain stopped and motioned to his men, signaling them to stay well to the side of the entrance.

If anyone was inside, he didn't want to make his crew an easy target. They were now at the entrance and still there was no sight or sound of anyone inside. Finally the captain said, "Well, men. There's no doubt that someone lives here. But since no one is home, shall we go in and look around?"

"We came this far, Captain. We can't stop now."

"Okay, which one wants to go in with me?" the Captain asked.

Everyone raised his hand. He turned and pointed to one of them.

"If we run into trouble inside, I'll fire one shot, so come and get us out." They nodded in agreement and with that, the two walked inside.

"Captain, look at this. It's like a fort in here. Weapons, equipment, even a jail cell! What do you make of it?"

"I'll tell you one thing. It belongs to Japan... or it did at one time," the captain answered. "And I'll tell you something else. This goes back to World War II. But someone still lives here, so we better get the hell out of here, till we find out who that someone is."

"I'm with you, Captain. Let's go."

He took another look around and then they hurried outside. "Come on, men, let's fall back into the jungle and talk this situation over." Everyone followed him back away from the cave quite some distance. When he felt it was a safe distance, he called them together. Everyone wanted to know what they found.

"This is all Jap equipment around here and there's no doubt someone lives here. Do you think it's some Jap holdout from the war?" one man asked.

"That's my guess," he answered. "We'll set up a watch from here and take turns with the binoculars. Sooner or later, someone's going to come back to the cave and I want some distance between them and us." He handed the binoculars to one man and told the rest to get comfortable. "This might be a long wait." The hours dragged on and still no sign of life. The Captain switched his radio on again and made contact with his radioman. Reporting they were all safe, he wanted to confirm there was, in fact, someone living on the island. They had an area under surveillance and would remain at this location for a few hours. If nothing developed, they would return to the ship before dark. The radioman acknowledged and then signaled off.

A few more hours passed and still no sign of life. The Captain was quietly telling the men to prepare to return to the ship when the man on the watch turned and said, "Bingo! Captain, someone just came home." He handed the glasses to the captain.

"You're right," he said, "there's one of them. He's standing at the cave entrance, looking around as if he suspects something." "What does he look like?" someone asked.

"Well, he's tall, with long hair and a beard."

"That doesn't sound like a description of a Jap to me," one of the men said.

"No, he's not Japanese. I'm sure of that. He's definitely a Caucasian. Who – and from where – I don't know. But there he stands, as big as life. Now he's going into the cave. I guess he didn't see anything disturbed. He must be satisfied everything's okay."

"Now what, Captain? Where do we go from here?"

"It's getting late. We'll go back to the ship and make some plans and come back early in the morning. We have to talk to this fellow somehow and find out what the hell's going on." With great care not to make noise, they started out through the jungle towards the beach to where their boats were hidden. When they had the boats off the beach and well out to sea, they started the engine and went back to the ship.

That night, everyone was talking about the man they had seen on the island, wondering how he got there and how many other people might be with him. Their guesses ranged from a shipwreck to an airliner going down. They studied the chart of the area again. No question, this is a very desolate part of the South Pacific. From this location all the way to New Guinea, there were thousands of islands and nearly all were uninhabited. They all knew after tomorrow they would be pulling anchor and moving on, with or without the answer to this mystery.

At the first light of dawn, they had their boats loaded and were heading once again back to the little island. After quietly reaching the beach they unloaded the boats, secured them, and started inland towards the cave. The plan was to split into two groups with everyone well armed. They would take up positions on each side of the cave entrance. Then with a bullhorn, the Captain would call for anyone inside to come out, in a friendly manner, they hoped. About half-an-hour later everything was set. The Captain said, "Well, here goes. Attention! Inside the cave! If there is anyone in there, please come out, without your weapons. We mean no harm. We just want to talk. We are Americans, exploring for oil in the area." They waited in silence quite some time. The captain looked at his men and shrugged his shoulders. "I guess there is no one home," he said. "Give me the light and cover me as well as you can. I'm going in."

"Captain! Don't move! We have company!" The captain turned and looked back. There stood the tall, bearded man behind them with a rifle pointed directly at him. Everyone froze in position. There was total silence for several moments. Finally the Captain said, "Okay, men – everyone drop their weapons. I don't want any heroes here. If we play our cards right, maybe no one will get hurt."

After dropping their weapons, everyone raised their arms in a gesture of surrender. The man motioned them to walk towards the beach. With the jungle quite dense, it was some time before they reached the water's edge. Once there, everyone looked out at the ship lying at anchor a short distance out. The man just stood there, looking at the ship. The American flag was visible. Then suddenly the man just dropped the rifle and stood there as if in a daze. They all just looked at each other, not knowing what to do next.

"Are you an American?" the Captain asked. It was as if the man could not hear him. He just stood there. Then the Captain told the men to go over and get the boat, but not to make any sudden moves. "There is something wrong here, and we're getting the hell out. Maybe he will come with us; but with or without him, we're leaving." The men went and brought the boat over to where the man and their Captain stood. All this time the man just stood there, and kept looking at the ship. They all climbed in the boat and the Captain reached out his hand and pulled on the man's arm. He slowly got into the boat and sat down, still not saying anything. They started the engines and headed out to the ship. As they neared the ship, their small craft was getting battered severely as the sea was becoming quite rough. By all indications, the good weather they had enjoyed for two weeks in the area was about to come to an end. When finally they were all safely back on board ship, the Captain ordered food and dry clothing for everyone. Surprisingly, their guest didn't seem very hungry. He did, however, drink a lot of milk; refused a beer; but accepted a soda. He appeared to be in relatively good health, but was still either unwilling or unable to communicate. The man remained a puzzling mystery to them all.

The ship's doctor and the Captain went to his quarters where the Captain told him everything that had happened up to this point. "Is there anyone else on the island?" the doctor asked.

"I don't think so, but we don't really know for sure. I felt it best to bring him on board; head for the nearest deep-water port and notify the authorities and then contact the nearest military base for them to take over."

"Do you think he's an American?" the doctor asked.

"I'd say either an Aussie or an American?" the Captain answered. "You see, everything we found on the island was Japanese – everything but the partial remains of an American airplane – something Lockheed built. We found several tags on some of the pieces."

"If it was a Jap base, and if he was shot down – where did everyone else go?"

"Damned if I know, doctor. The whole thing is weird... like... why won't he talk? He hasn't said a damn word. Yet, healthwise, he seems okay."

The doctor took a deep breath. "Maybe he was in that plane when it crashed and got banged around pretty bad. Could be a head injury. You never know. When we get back to civilization they can run a series of tests on him; but maybe it's just an act."

The Captain said, "I know for sure he can see and hear. We'll keep on him all the way back to port. If he's bluffing, we'll catch him."

The doctor nodded in agreement. "Keep an eye on him. I'm going to check with the navigator to see which port is closest and how long it will take to get there." In a few minutes their decision was made. After studying the charts, they would head for Port Moresby. They were less than thirty hours away. There was an airfield there. They could notify Naval Headquarters at Hawaii. They in turn could send a plane and pick the man up and take over the situation from there. The captain would provide the authorities with the location of the island in case they wanted to check it out or look for more survivors. Twenty-eight hours later the ship dropped anchor in Port Moresby. The Captain went directly to the port authorities and immediately notified Naval Headquarters. They, in turn, checked with Air Force and learned that they had several aircraft in the area. They would send transport in and pick the man up within hours.

In the meantime, the captain made his report to his home office of the oil company, relating all the activities of the last forty-eight hours. The California-based oil company lost no time in contacting the news media. Releasing the story of how one of their ships had made a bizarre rescue of a man believed to be an American. It brought a swarm of reporters from all the news companies. They clamored for more details but all that could be added was the fact that the man was in the custody of the US Air Force and was being flown back to Edwards Air Base in California.

Chapter Twenty

Robin was now eighteen and had just passed her driving test. Lowie promised, if she succeeded on her first attempt, to take her on a weekend trip up the coast of New England, and the new driver could do much of the driving. With that as a goal, Robin studied and practiced diligently. The end result was a triumph for her. She especially wanted to visit Mystic Harbor. So on a Friday, the two packed their bags and that afternoon, left for New England.

Saturday morning arrived with bright sun and clear skies. The air from the sea was cool and the trees in the area were dressed in bright red and gold. It was a near perfect autumn day. That day was spent at Mystic Harbor. Sunday was going to be spent visiting the little fishing towns along the coast.

They were up early Sunday morning and the first town on their agenda was the little village of Stonington. With its stately homes and antique shops, it was like a picture postcard. As Robin drove down the narrow street, she saw a sign which read "Stonington Point" and an arrow indicating straight ahead. They followed the street which took them out on a little pier. Stopping the car, they sat there a long time, watching the waves rolling in, crashing on the big rocks below. The wind was now quite strong and it tossed the little fishing boats about, making the job of the men on board quite difficult. They were gathering their lobster traps. "Let's get out a while," Robin said.

As Lowie got out and started around the front of the car, she heard the big flag flapping in the wind and looked up at the flagpole. At that moment it all came back to her. She called out, "Robin! This must be it!"

"What, Mother? What is it?" Robin asked as she came back to the car.

"This place. It must be the place Doug told me about. He was here once when he was stationed in the area, and it really impressed him. He said if anything ever happened to him, sometime I should come to this spot. It's so beautiful. I hate to leave it. He told me to stand here by the sea and listen real hard. I might hear someone call my name and if I do, it would be him. It all happened so long ago and I had nearly forgotten it, but here I stand at what, I'm sure, is the very spot he told me about. He was right, I could stay here forever. Sorry, Robin, this must sound pretty silly. But I…"

"No, Mother," Robin cut in, "I think it's beautiful and I'm glad you share some of those kind of moments out of your life with me."

They stood with their arms around each other watching the gulls circling the fishing boats. The waves were rolling in and crashing hard on the big boulders just below them. The wind was getting quite cold now and Lowie said, "I guess we better get back in the car before we freeze." They were sitting in the car watching the little fishing boats bobbing up and down in the rough sea as the men struggled with their lobster traps.

After some time Robin asked, "Shall we continue with our journey?" Her mother nodded her head in agreement. They both felt a little sad to leave this village they had fallen in love with so quickly. She drove up from the little pier and as she turned on to the narrow street leading out of town, Lowie turned and took one last look back. "We'll come back Mother, we'll come back here often."

"It's just as Doug said it was," her mother answered quietly. "He was right. I really do love this area."

They spent most of the day following the old road north, along the ocean, as it wound its way through several fishing villages; each one like a picture come alive. They spent the rest of the day visiting antique shops and gift stores. As the evening approached, Robin turned south and started back to their motel at Mystic Harbor.

Being quite late when they arrived, they were now preparing for bed. Robin turned the TV on for a weather report. A few moments later the network interrupted the program in progress to announce a news bulletin. The newscaster started his announcement with, "I have just received a bulletin stating a man has been found on an island in the South Pacific. He is believed to be an American who has been marooned; possibly since World War II. He is being flown back to Edwards Air Base in California. We will give all the details as they become available to us, and now… we return you to our regularly scheduled program already in progress."

Lowie sat down on the edge of the bed. She was trembling as

she looked at Robin. "Dear God in heaven!" she cried. "Could it be Doug? Do you think it could really be him?"

"Yes, Mother, it's possible but please don't get your hopes up."

"I can't help it, Robin. I'm so nervous I'm trembling. We have to go home. Let's go home right now."

"Okay, Mother, I'll get everything packed. We can leave right away."

They listened to the radio all the way home. There was little added to the story, except that the plane was expected to arrive at Edwards Air Base some time the next day.

By ten o'clock the following morning, all the networks were carrying the story. They were all giving live coverage from Edwards Air Base. Lowie and Robin watched as the plane taxied up to the gate where an ambulance was waiting. The plane came to a stop and, after several long and agonizing moments for Lowie, the door finally was opened. When the steps were in place, two men came out; then a third. This man was tall and thin, wearing white coveralls. His beard and hair were quite long and it was obvious it had been black but now was turning gray. The two men helped him down the steps and as they got into the ambulance, a mob of news people were frantically trying to get close-up shots as they shouted questions; which all went unanswered.

Robin looked at Lowie who was sitting in front of the TV and said, "Was it Doug?"

"I don't know. I couldn't tell. Just look at me. I'm shaking all over." Just then a newsman explained the man's identity was not known as yet. The Air Force was going to run print checks as soon as the man's health could be known. It was reported the man could not speak. Also, his identity would not be released until his next-of-kin could be notified. Two hours later there was an update to the drama that was unfolding. They reported the man's physical condition was good. However, he could not speak and seemed unable to comprehend anything around him. At this point, the doctors were puzzled as to why this condition existed.

That afternoon, Lowie went to her office at the agency. Her father had heard the accounts of the man, and like everyone, was interested in the story. They talked about it for some time. He warned his daughter that the chances of this man being her friend were very remote.

"I know that, Dad, but I still can't stop hoping it is him. It is this not knowing that is driving me insane."

"I just don't want to see you get your hopes up and then be hurt all over again," her dad said.

"I know, Dad, but I promise, if it turns out that way, I'll handle my disappointment. But till they release his name, I'm going to continue hoping it's Doug."

That evening she and Robin were waiting for the six thirty news. The lead story on all the networks was of the man and his identity. The newscaster started his broadcast with, "Good evening, everyone. It is now official. The man found on a South Pacific island was positively identified. He is, in fact, an American." At that moment Lowie grabbed Robin's arm and held on, hardly breathing. She closed her eyes as the man continued. "He was a Captain in the Army Air Force during World War II. His name has been verified as one Douglas Stewart from Pennsylvania, where some of his family has been reached."

At this moment Lowie threw her arms around Robin and started to laugh and cry at the same time, saying over and over "Thank you Dear God in heaven. Thank you."

"The information we have at the moment," the newscaster continued, "indicates Captain Stewart survived a plane crash and lived on a deserted island in the Pacific. Whether it was occupied by the Japanese at the time, is not certain, but it is believed Captain Stewart is the sole survivor. By all indications, he has been marooned for nearly thirty years. The Air Force is trying, at this time, to confirm these reports with Washington. They have been unable to unravel Captain Stewart's life to this point because of his complete inability to communicate with the doctors on the scene. We can, however, show the viewing audience Captain Stewart without his beard and long hair, thanks to the efforts of our reporter on the scene, just outside the base barber shop, where he was able to file this report."

For the first time, since they had said their goodbyes at the airport the night Doug left to return to his outfit, Lowie actually saw the man she had promised to wait for and he was just as handsome as she remembered. "It's really him, Robin, it's Doug! I can't believe it – after all these years – I can't believe this is really happening."

"Can I go with you?" Robin asked. "You are going to whatever hospital they take him to aren't you?"

"Yes, I certainly am. Nothing can stop me from going wherever he is. I'll call his brother. I think he lives in the Harrisburg area someplace. After Doug's parents died, I sort of dropped out of his family's life. That was nearly ten years ago."

The next morning she went through the Harrisburg telephone directory and checked the listing of Stewarts. There was only one of Doug's brothers listed – "John C Stewart." She called at about seven thirty and in answer to the caller's question – yes, he was in fact a brother of Douglas Stewart.

"Hi, John! It's me, Lowie Meese – remember?"

"Lowie! Of course I remember you. As soon as the Air Force called us I thought of you and wondered whatever became of you. Are you married?"

"No, I never did get married. I guess the right guy just never came along. The reason I called, I wondered if it would be possible for me to visit Doug?"

"Of course, Lowie. We were hoping you would want to. It might be the best thing in the world for him. The doctors told us they are completely at a loss as to why he can't speak or comprehend anything. Physically, he seems to be in fine shape. They are moving him to Walter Reed Hospital in Washington. That will make it easier for his family to be with him. He's a man who's been in a void for nearly thirty years. There's no telling what he has gone through. The doctors say, maybe, familiar voices and faces around him might help. The government is sending a team back to the island to search for more survivors and try to piece together what might have happened on that island."

"Will you call me when you know Doug is at Walter Reed?"

"Of course; where can I reach you?"

She gave him her telephone numbers at her home and at her office. The next two days it was difficult for her to concentrate on her job. Every time the phone rang she answered quickly, hoping it would be John with the news she was waiting for. Finally that call came.

John told her the government notified him Douglas was now at Walter Reed and he could have visitors. He was also warned not to expect too much. The doctors were having little success with Doug's condition as yet, but they were optimistic, he told her. He was leaving in the morning for Washington and she was more than welcome to go along with him and his wife. She quickly accepted the invitation and after thanking him for his kindness and consideration said goodbye.

She then called her parents and gave them the news. Her dad volunteered to take over the business while she was gone. That night she told Robin everything that had happened so far and explained that it would be best if she didn't go along this first visit since she was going with John and his wife. But if everything went well, the two of them would spend the next weekend together in Washington.

It was a restless night for her. She was much too excited to fall asleep, just thinking about tomorrow and her first meeting with the man she loved and hadn't seen for nearly thirty years.

It was almost noon when John and his wife and Lowie arrived at Walter Reed Hospital. They went first to the information desk and asked for Doctor Farr. He was the doctor who had been in constant contact with John. He and two other doctors were assigned to Doug's care. It was but a few moments after being paged that Doctor Farr arrived in the lounge. After the introductions, he asked everyone to sit down as he wanted to bring them up to date. The three doctors had been working with Doug for several days now and these things they knew for certain. First, Captain Stewart was in very good physical condition. He was, however, unable to speak or comprehend anything. His eyesight was normal, and he seemed to be in no pain.

"Doctor Farr," John asked, "is this a type of amnesia?"

The doctor shook his head. "I would have to say, not really. You see, an amnesia victim usually is quite normal in his present life – but has no recollection of the past. The Captain's problem in a sense, is he hasn't the ability to communicate."

"Doctor Farr," Lowie asked, "what are the possibilities of having a breakthrough with Doug's condition?"

He looked at her for a moment and then said, "I don't want to raise false hopes, but I feel there's a key to unlocking his memory and we must try everything possible to do just that. I understand you were to be married when the Captain came home. I wonder if it would be possible for you to work with us? Your presence might be a very helpful addition for us."

"Doctor Farr, for Doug I'll do anything you think might help; starting today and for the rest of my life if need be."

"Thank you, I was hoping you would feel this way. I don't

know how long it will take to reach Douglas, but I feel sure it won't be that long. We're looking for a key element here and you might be a tremendous asset in helping us reach the goal we all want. Now I think it best his brother goes into his room first. Please don't become discouraged with these first few meetings. This man has been out of civilization for many years, and the world has changed so dramatically in that time, that even a person with all their faculties would be in awe and amazement with the startling changes the world has gone through. Just spend time with him. Don't force any issues and please don't become emotional. Speak quietly and keep the conversation about things of the past. I want all of you to let him know you are just good friends and you have all been separated for a long time. The hearing problem he seems to be having may be an emotional condition. It's just one of the many things, at this time, we don't know. So when you speak to him, keep this in mind. We're not certain of anything with his condition. He may be able to hear parts, or maybe all, of your conversation. We just don't know. For now, that's all. So please cooperate with me on this."

"Of course, Doctor; whatever you say. We're all here for the same thing; hopefully to help."

"Thank you, John. You and your wife may go in now."

They slowly opened the door and entered Doug's room. He was sitting on the edge of the bed. The beard was gone and his hair was cut short. John knew instantly it was his brother, Doug. He walked over, reached out and took his hand. Not knowing quite what to say, he just simply said, "Hi, Buddy. It's been a long time. Welcome home. You probably don't recognize me. The last time you saw me I was about forty pounds lighter. We were just scrawny kids then. Boy, you look great! Wish I was as lean and trim as you are. As they say, the old middle-age spread caught up with me," he joked. Doug slowly got up from the bed. He stood for a moment and looked towards his brother and then suddenly all expression left his face and his eyes were blank. He said nothing; then walked slowly over to the window and looked out. John looked at his wife and as tears came to his eyes, he said, "We better go now." She nodded in agreement. They returned to the lounge where Lowie and the doctor were waiting.

As they entered, Lowie was standing, looking out of the window. She turned, and in a near whisper asked, "Did he know you?" John stood looking at her a moment and then shook his head to say "no".

"I'm sorry Lowie. There was no response at all. I just can't believe it. He seems so healthy and he really looks great, yet he shows no expression at all. It's as if he never saw me before."

"May I go in now, Doctor?" she asked.

"Of course, but please be careful. Remember, he has no recall of the past at all, as yet. You may stay with him as long as you wish. I'll wait here. I want to go over all the reports again, from the time he was first spotted until now. I want to make sure I'm not overlooking anything. We'll talk after your visit with him."

"Thank you, Doctor. I promise I won't stay long."

She walked down the hall and stopped at Doug's door. Standing with her hand on the door, she was both frightened and excited. Pushing the door open, she quickly stepped inside. She was so nervous she was trembling. It was like a dream for her. Standing across the room, looking out of the window was the handsome man she had fallen so desperately in love with, so many years ago. And she knew instantly that love had never died. It was like a miracle for her. She wanted to run over and throw her arms around him and never let go, but she remembered the doctor's advice. Trying to stay calm, she softly said, "Hello, dear heart. Welcome home. I still love you and I missed you every minute you've been gone." She walked over to the window where he was standing. Her hand trembled as she reached for his hand. She stood quietly by his side and then put her arm around him. With her head resting against his arm, she closed her eyes, and all those lonely years melted away and the memories she shared with Doug came flooding back in a warm glow. "I love you, Doug," she whispered, as she fought back the tears. He made no response at all. She stood looking up into his eyes for a long time. His expression never changed. He just stood there, staring out of the window. From time to time he would close his eyes for a few moments and then open them again as if trying to think. But then a blank expression would return. She stayed with him for half-an-hour and found it very difficult to leave, even though she knew she would be with him every day from now on if the doctors would allow it. She tenderly kissed his hand and then forced herself to leave the room. Once in the hall, she burst into tears. The others were still in the lounge when she got back. The four sat and went over everything. As they spoke, the doctor made more entries in the log he was compiling. He was sure it would eventually help him unlock the Captain's mind.

In the weeks that followed, Lowie spent every evening with Doug at the hospital. They usually took long walks around the hospital grounds. Sometimes they just sat on a bench and she would take his hand and talk quietly to him. She told him about their times together in Texas and when he came back from overseas injured; how she had met him in California; how they spent a brief time together; and then he had to return to duty overseas again. These conversations left her frustrated and nearly always in tears for the results were always the same; just a blank stare into the distance from Doug. The doctor kept in constant touch with her and as always, took notes of their conversation.

On her next visit, Lowie took one of Doug's letters with her. At what she thought was the right time, she read the letter to him. It was the first letter of his she had received from overseas. Just as she finished reading, he turned slowly and looked directly into her eyes and for a brief moment there was a sparkle in his dark blue eyes. She held her breath, not wanting to disrupt his possible flash of recall. But then just as quickly, the blank stare returned and his mind slipped away again. After her visit, Lowie hurried home and called the doctor. She was very excited as she told him of Doug's first glimpse of response. The doctor was quite impressed and suggested she continue to read one letter each visit, being careful to note any response; particularly what portion of the letters would trigger such a reaction. They might find some particular passages which would help Doug reach a breakthrough.

As the days passed, the doctor continued his treatment and different experiments with Doug. Lowie always looked forward to her visits, always hoping this day would be the day she would get her Doug back; hoping he would say, "Hi, honey, I'm home." But each visit left her troubled and saddened. One thing she knew – she would never give up. She and the doctor would meet several times a week and go over every detail. The doctor was most impressed with her ability to, at times, briefly touch on a line or passage in her letters that would generate a fleeting spark of response. Doctor Farr questioned her at length about their earlier romance. He explained he had a plan involving her if she could spend the time with the captain. She told him she would make the time. Nothing, now or in the past, was more important to her than Doug. The doctor looked at her for a moment and then said, "I've made no progress with Doug – and I've tried all types of treatment. In fact, you have made more progress with your visits once a day than I have with constant therapy. With this in mind, would it be possible for you to travel with Doug to Texas? I would like to take him back to the area where you and he met and spent time together. I would need at least a week of your time. I can't promise anything, but I feel the experiment should be tried. Can you do it?"

"Gladly, Doctor. There's nothing I would rather do. When can we leave?"

"I'll make the arrangements tomorrow. When everything is finalized, I'll call you."

"Thank you, Doctor Farr. We all appreciate your efforts and concern for Doug."

"No thanks are necessary. First, it's my job and let's say I like my occupation; and second, I owe this man and all his comrades more than I could ever pay. As I see it, it's men like the Captain that made our lives possible. I'm honored that in a small way I am able to help."

The following day the doctor called Lowie at her office. He explained the arrangements he had made with the Pentagon. They would have a plane at his disposal the following day. It would be coming into Andrews Air Force Base at ten o'clock in the morning. Would there be any problem with that for her? Could she make it? She quickly assured him she would be there, ready to go. It was to be another sleepless night. She was looking forward to this new attempt in the doctor's treatment program. The next day she arrived at Andrews and found the doctor, his nurse, and Doug already there. The Air Force plane that was to take them to Kelly Field in Texas taxied towards the gate where they were waiting. The doctor introduced her to the nurse who was assigned to go along, and would be with them the entire trip, which could best be explained as an experiment. As the doctor was talking to them, Doug was standing nearby with his hands resting on his hips and Lowie could see the now familiar puzzled expression on his face. He was watching each plane as they were coming in and taking off. He would close his eyes a moment, then open them, turn his head from side to side, and then start to raise his hand as if to gesture. Then just as suddenly drop it to his side as if the frustration was too much to bear. Every time she saw him do this, it nearly broke her heart. She quickly went to his side, took hold of his arm and held on tightly. She fought to hold back the tears. She had seen him do this several times and each time, she so desperately wanted to say or do something that would break the barrier, he seemed to be trying to bridge; but each time it ended the same way. Just more bitter heartaches. Within the hour, they boarded the plane and were on their way to Texas. Shortly after take-off Doug had fallen asleep. She sat by his side, holding his hand as he seemed to be totally exhausted. She leaned over, kissed his cheek and whispered, "Dear God, when he awakens, please let this nightmare end." A short time later, with her head resting against Doug, she too, fell asleep.

There was a staff car waiting for them when they landed at Kelly Field. They went first to the base hospital where Doug was to undergo more tests the following day. Lowie and the nurse shared an apartment on the base. The doctor stayed at the BOQ. He had requested and received a period of two weeks to work with Doug on what he felt might be the most stable memory period the Captain had experienced. With Lowie completing those exciting times from the young man's life, he felt her constant presence might, in some way, be constructive with his planned experimental treatments. The success of life and memory restoration was possible.

At the end of the first week, Doug seemed tired. Lowie spent several hours each day with him, walking to familiar areas. They started their revisiting journeys with a stop at the store where they had first met. And from there, she traced their happy memories of so long ago, but with little visible response from Doug. There were moments when her hopes would nearly explode. One such time, they were out at the old parade grounds and Doug turned and looked towards the bleachers then slowly looked down into her eyes. For a brief moment those eyes she knew so well flashed a kind of spark and her heart nearly stopped. She just stood there, holding his hand. With tears welling up in her eyes, she managed to smile at him, squeezing his hand even harder, but then just as quickly, that spark disappeared and his expression returned to the dreaded blank, she now knew so well. The pain and frustration was taking its toll on her also. Trying desperately not to cry, she turned, and they started back to the hospital. That night, she sat down with the doctor and the nurse to review everything that had taken place that first week. She was surprised the doctor was impressed. She told him she had hoped for so much more. He again explained to her, even with all their efforts, a breakthrough for Doug might never come, but none of them must ever give up. With that she agreed, then apologized for sounding impatient. "I feel so sorry for Doug. He seems to try so hard at times and then it's like he has pain in his head. He'll just cover his eyes with his hands and shake his head back and forth and a moment later, the blank expression returns to his face. Then sometimes he just turns and walks away from me as if this world doesn't even exist. We've got to do more, Doctor. We must do more, somehow."

"Believe me, miss, I'm not about to give up on this man. We have another week here, but if we don't make any progress in this experiment, I'll take him back to Walter Reed and start electro-shock treatments if I must."

"I hope it never comes to that," she said. "I'm no doctor, but that thought scares me."

"You needn't be frightened of any treatment or experiments I use while working with this man. I can assure you I would never conduct any treatments that would endanger him in any way."

"I'm sure you wouldn't, Doctor. It's just that I love him so and it frightens me to think he has slipped away from this life and I may never get him back."

"Try not to think of that. Tomorrow we move on to other areas around here where you two spent quiet times together. You were telling me of a park area. Didn't you say that's where he spent the last few evenings before shipping out?"

"Yes. We would sit on the bench and plan our future and watch the sunsets. It was so peaceful and quiet there. It's where he always wanted to go to unwind after a hectic day of flight training."

"Okay, tomorrow evening we'll take him back to that spot and you spend an hour or so with him. Talk about anything you feel that might make an impression. In dealing with a condition like this, there are no textbook answers. No one has any factual guidelines. We in the medical profession have only theories; so feel free to say or do whatever you, as his closest friend, feel best at the moment."

"I'll continue to do the very best I can, Doctor."

The next three days were repetitions of the past days. The doctor conducted more experiments and tests during the day and

Lowie spent the evening with him. As the days wore on, she again worried if they were doing the right thing. At times, Doug seemed even more tired and confused. She spoke again to the doctor about her concerns. He pleaded with her to try it one more day. She looked at the doctor and said, "I hope the Good Lord strikes me dead if I'm doing the wrong thing."

He said, "I can assure you, what you're doing is the right thing."

The next evening, the doctor brought Doug to the park a little early. He parked the car at the bottom of the hill, went around and opened the door for Doug. They walked up the winding path a short distance. The doctor stopped and stood there a few minutes, watching Doug as he continued on up the path. A little later Lowie arrived. It was obvious she had been crying.

"Is there any change today?"

The doctor slowly shook his head, "No". He took her hand and said, "Please, let's go up to the top of the hill. He's standing up there watching the sunset."

"No, Doctor, please! He can't remember me. He can't remember anything. You have tried. Others have tried. I've tried so often the last two weeks. We've put him through so much. It must be torture for him. He can't speak. He doesn't know who we are. He doesn't know who he is or where he is or where he has been all these years."

Tears were in her eyes as she pleaded with the doctor, but slowly they walked back up the hill. The sun's rays had just touched the low clouds, as they neared the graying men standing alone, looking to the West. Just then the sky burst out in bright gold and gray. It was too beautiful to describe. She reached out and took his hand. She looked up into his eyes and her thoughts raced back nearly thirty years. That evening was just like this one; two kids stood holding hands, watching a sunset; an evening the pretty little girl would never forget (nor the dark-haired boy she clung to so tightly) both knowing their parting was now, and maybe forever. As she looked into those eyes, they appeared completely blank. Then with tears streaming down her cheeks, she said, "Douglas Stewart, I love you. I love you; now as I did years and years ago. I have never stopped loving you and I never will. Please give me some sign you know what I'm saying." He withdrew his hands, turned, and slowly walked away.

114

The doctor ran to her side and said, "Go with him. Please, lady, go with him."

Sobbing, she said, "Doctor, I can't do it any more. I can't torture him. He's in his other world and we can't bring him back. I've lost him. We've all lost him. He's back with us, but he's not home. He can't find his way back. For him, the man I've loved all my life, it's a blank. He can't find it. For him, there is no road back."

The doctor put his arm around her. "I'm sorry," he said. "I'm sorry I couldn't do more. We'll leave in the morning. I'll take him back to Walter Reed Hospital." They walked over to where Doug was standing. "Damn! I hate to fail," the doctor complained. "I never was a good loser. I'm so damn frustrated! I feel like going out and getting drunk."

"Don't blame yourself, Doctor. We all know you have tried very hard and we really appreciate it. No one wanted to see you succeed more than I. I've prayed for his return from the day his plane went down... and I'll keep on praying for us all..." she said, her voice falling off to a whisper.

The next morning, they boarded the plane and started the flight back to Washington. The return flight was very quiet in comparison with the flight out. No one could hide their bitter disappointment. When they left Walter Reed everyone was so optimistic; but now on returning, the mood was realized as another defeat. Doug was sitting at a window with Lowie by his side, holding onto his arm. Feeling emotionally drained from the preceding days, she laid her head back, closed her eyes and in moments was asleep.

After arriving in Washington, the doctor returned with Doug to Walter Reed. Lowie checked into a hotel close by. It was quite late and she was very tired and depressed. Her hopes of getting Doug back were now left in shambles. After all the years of waiting, was this the way it must end? She sat down on the bed and burst into tears. "Dear God, help me," she cried, "I can't let go."

The next morning, she called the doctor to tell him she was going back home to Pennsylvania. She had to get back to her business, but she would keep in touch and come back to the hospital to visit Doug every weekend. He thanked her for her assistance and again apologized for not being able to help Douglas. He assured her, if there were any breakthroughs, he would call her personally. After their goodbyes, Lowie started the drive north back to Harrisburg.

In a few hours, she was again home. That night, she told Robin and her parents all that had happened in the last two weeks, with everything ending in complete failure. "All of my hopes and expectations," she told them, "have now turned to doubts and fears."

Just then the telephone rang and Robin answered it. A moment later she interrupted her mother and said, "It's for you. It's Doug's doctor. He's calling from the hospital."

Lowie's voice trembled as she said, "Hello. This is Lowie Meese. Is anything wrong?" She listened a moment and then said, "Are you sure? Of course, I'll be there in the morning. But are you sure? Please doctor, don't get my hopes up unless you're absolutely sure. There have been so many disappointments. I don't think I can endure another one." She listened intently for a few moments and then said, "Thank you doctor, I truly am grateful that you called. Thank you again, and I'll be there in the morning." After saying goodbye, she carefully put the receiver back on the telephone. With her face showing the seriousness of the conversation, she said, "The doctor just told me there was a mix-up in the x-ray room and he was given someone else's x-rays. They were supposed to have been Doug's. As soon as he was aware of this, he ordered new x-rays and what he found was shocking."

"What is it?" her dad asked.

"They found a metal object that has penetrated his skull and it's imbedded in a portion of his brain. They are going to operate tomorrow. The doctor has contacted Doug's family and his brother will be there tomorrow morning. He wanted me to come down also. The medical team would like to go over the surgery they will be performing on Doug. They're sure of its success but they want us to understand the risks involved with brain surgery and they have no idea what his reaction will be after the operation. They seem optimistic but we will all have to wait and hope for the best, of course." They talked about this for quite some time, as she prepared to leave early in the morning for Washington.

Upon her arrival the next morning, she was escorted to a conference room and found everyone already there. The chief surgeon explained the forthcoming operation, showing them the x-rays and drawing diagrams of what must be done. They had determined the object was an ordinary nail and it had been driven in with considerable force. It was not visible on the external because the scalp had healed over the area completely. The surgeon told them if the operation was successful, there was a good chance Doug's condition could be restored; maybe completely. Of course, no one could be certain of that. He went on to explain and asked them not to worry. The operation would take hours and it could be hours after the surgery, before they would know anything. But they would be notified of the results immediately. Lowie decided to stay at the closest hotel and wait out the ordeal as best she could.

It was ten twenty the following day, when the telephone in her hotel room started to ring. Her hand shook as she raised the receiver to her ear. She was terrified as to what she might hear. "Hello. Is this Lowie Meese?"

"Yes it is," she quickly answered.

"This is Doctor Madison. The operation on Captain Stewart was a success and he is resting comfortably now. It will be twelve to fourteen hours before we begin to know of how much success the surgery is."

"When can I see him?" she asked.

The doctor was silent for a few moments and then said, "I would guess in another forty-eight hours. It all depends on his mental reactions. The psychiatrist will be working with him on his recovery; for there will be a tremendous readjustment period. To the best of our knowledge, this man is coming back to a world he knows little about. With all the changes in the world that have taken place in the last thirty years, it may be a traumatic experience for him."

"Would it be possible for someone to call me when it's okay for Doug to have visitors?" she asked.

"Of course," the doctor answered. "I'll call you myself – no problem. Well, I must go," he said. "I'll be in touch very soon. Take care and try not to worry."

"Thank you doctor, thank you all for everything," she answered.

It was four o'clock the following day before she heard from the hospital. Doctor Madison called and asked her to come to the hospital. He wanted to bring her up to date on everything that had been accomplished so far, and he assured her there was a lot of good news. When she arrived at the hospital, Doug's brother introduced her to the rest of the family. They had all come to Washington with high hopes that their brother would be back home with them at last. A nurse directed them all into a waiting room in which Doctor Madison was waiting. He used a copy of the x-ray to explain what they found and how the operation was performed. As it turned out, the metal object was indeed, a common nail such as those used in wood construction. Somehow it had been driven through his skull and penetrated the brain in such a way that it did minimal tissue damage. What it did do (in a sense) was cause what could be termed a short circuit of some of the nerve ends. Had it been a fraction of an inch to the right or left, it would have, in all probability, meant instant death. Through the years, the body had formed a gristle tissue around it; thereby protecting the delicate cells in that area. This, in turn, caused more pressure on the nerve tissues of the speech and memory section of the brain.

"I'm happy to say," the doctor went on, "the operation was 100 percent successful and Doug's recovery is well on its way. I do, however, want to caution you all, his readjustment to a world with all these years of changes might be anything but easy. I'm sure the Captain will overcome this obstacle, too, with everyone's help and understanding. My friends," the doctor smiled, "this is quite a guy we have here. Now I'm sure you didn't come to Walter Reed to listen to me ramble on and on. We're going to allow Doug visitors today. I would suggest the brothers go in two at a time and not stay very long. If Doug wants to talk, good; but if not, then keep the conversation light and don't ask him a lot of questions. I just want to add, I'm sure his recovery will be total and complete with time."

As they started down the corridor to Doug's room, Doctor Madison came over to Lowie. With tears in her eyes, she said, "Doctor Madison, I'm so happy I can't believe this is happening. I want to thank you and all the doctors for making this miracle complete."

Smiling, the doctor bowed, then humbly said, "I thank God we had enough skill to make it a success. I haven't eaten anything today yet, and while the family is visiting the Captain, I wonder if you would join me at the cafeteria? It would give us some time to talk a few things over."

"Thank you, Doctor, I'd like that very much," she said.

When they arrived, the cafeteria was nearly empty. After selecting some food they sat down at a table close to a window. The doctor asked how long she had known Doug. "We met when he was a flight cadet," she said, "and it was love nearly from the beginning. We spent every minute together we could, and when he left it was a constant flow of letters. I had no interest in other men for he meant everything to me and I was more than willing to wait. I already had the best – how could I do better? And if he is half as great as the fellow I fell in love with, I'll still be the luckiest woman in this world." She sat there looking out the window and then as if in thinking out loud, she whispered, "I'm scared." She turned and looked at the doctor. "I'm scared, Doctor Madison, I'm so nervous, I'm shaking."

"It's quite natural," he answered. "It's been a long time. You have changed. The world has changed. And this man has been through hell. It won't be easy. Don't expect everything to fall into place."

"Oh, I don't expect any of it to be easy for a long time. I just hope we can salvage some of what's left of our lives."

The doctor reached across the table to hold her hand. He said, "I'll go in first and break the news to the Captain that the prettiest little lady out of his past is nervously waiting in the hall to visit him."

"But Doctor, what if he doesn't remember me? I wouldn't be able to take that. I'm serious. I'd go out of my mind."

The doctor squeezed her hand. "Don't worry – nobody could forget you – and I'm sure Doug will be just as nervous as you."

"But what should I say when I step through that door?" The doctor looked at her, smiled and said, "I'm sure you'll say the right thing. Love is like that. When he looks into your eyes, those years will all melt away and you'll be two kids again who can always kiss better than they can talk. Okay, lady – let's go visit the Captain."

As they walked down the long corridor neither spoke. Stopping at Room 22, Doctor Madison smiled and said, "You aren't going to faint when you walk through that door, are you?"

"Doctor I'm scared. It's nearly thirty years I've been waiting for this moment."

"Suppose you go and sit down for a few minutes. I'll go in and make sure Doug has no visitors. I'll talk to him a while and sort of set the stage for your entrance.

"Thanks Doctor. I was hoping you would say that."

"Relax a while. I'll be out in a few minutes." With that, the doctor entered the room.

Doug was lying in bed with his eyes closed. There was no one else in the room and it was very quiet. The doctor looked at him a few moments then quietly said, "Captain Stewart, it's Doctor Madison again. Do you feel like talking?"

Doug opened his eyes, turned and looked at the doctor. "Yes, Sir," he answered in a deep voice.

"So how are you feeling? Is there any pain?"

"Not much. But I'm having a hard time trying to get things straight in my mind. Some of my family just left. They said I am in a hospital in Washington DC. How did I get here? And what happened to the top of my head? I feel like I'm wearing a turban."

"You're recovering from an operation. It could have been very serious; but as it turned out, everything went very smoothly. You'll be out of here soon."

"They tell me I've been lost for a long time?"

"Well, Captain, it has indeed been a long time. But you're home now. Safe and sound."

Doug stared at the doctor in utter disbelief. "Doctor, you can't be serious. My God, what year is it?"

Doctor Madison sat down on the edge of the bed. "It's 1975. You were shot down in the Pacific during the war and survived on an island. Five weeks ago some men found you and the Air Force brought you back to the States. The team here at Walter Reed has been working with you ever since and I'm proud to say with a great deal of success."

"But Doctor!" he yelled, "the last date I remember is February, 1945. I was a squadron commander and we were planning a raid. Before we left I wrote a letter to my girl back in the States. I remember it was her birthday. It was February 1. For God's sake, Doctor, is this some kind of a joke or a bad dream? You can't be serious!"

"Yes, Captain, I'm very serious."

"Then you're telling me I lost thirty years of my life? What the hell do I do now? I'm an old man! How could this happen? Who won the damn war, anyway?"

"We did, Doug. It ended late in 1945."

Doug covered his eyes with his hands, as tears started to run down his cheeks. "Dear God in heaven, please help me. I'm lost, and I can't go on by myself. Clear my mind and give me strength. Why did this happen?" he shouted. "Why were all those years taken from me?"

Just then the nurse came in with his medication. She was followed by the psychiatrist. He looked at Doctor Madison and said, "That's all for today, Doctor. It's time for his nap. This has been a big day and now he needs a lot of rest."

"Okay, Captain, get some sleep and I'll see you tomorrow. We'll fill in some more of the blank spaces and I'll bring a special visitor with me tomorrow. Okay?"

"Okay, Doctor. And thanks. I'm sorry I yelled at you."

"No problem, Doug. Take care and get some sleep."

He closed the door quietly behind him and started down the hall to where Lowie was sitting. As he approached her, he said, "I'm sorry, but I'm afraid you'll not be able to visit the Captain today. He had too much of a busy schedule and now he needs some rest. But don't worry he's doing fine. I guess that's some of the problem," he continued, "he's doing too well. He's recalling too much, too fast. The psychiatrist would like a little slower pace. He's received his medication now and I told him I'd see him tomorrow and bring a special visitor."

"He is all right, isn't he Doctor? You're not just telling me this to hide something?"

"No, I wouldn't do something like that. I can assure you he's responding unbelievably well. You'll see when we come back tomorrow."

"What time should I come over to the hospital?"

"Make it about three o'clock in the afternoon. That will give the psychiatrist more time to talk to Doug. They're doing a great job helping him sort out some of the happenings that took place since he's been gone. It's truly a mind-boggling job. In their reports to me, they are amazed at Doug's complete acceptance of what must have been a horrifying experience for him."

"As I told you before, Doctor, Douglas Stewart is an exceptional person," she said, as a smile came over her face.

"You know, miss," the doctor replied, "I'm beginning to believe you." They said goodbye after agreeing on a three o'clock meeting the next day.

That night she called her daughter Robin to tell her she was going to talk to Doug for the first time tomorrow, and she was so excited she was afraid she wouldn't be able to sleep. They talked briefly about the happenings to that point and after promising to call her back the next day, they said goodbye.

The sun rose on a clear cool day and Lowie knew the waiting for three o'clock would be nerve-racking. Because of this, she decided to go shopping. She found herself looking for something special to wear. Something that would be just right. She smiled as she realized she wasn't shopping for herself, she was looking for something Doug might like. After all these years, the thought gave her a warm glow inside. After several hours, she arrived at her hotel, loaded down with packages. She spent time trying on two different outfits. She knew she was acting like a silly school girl but it was fun and exciting. She was going to see her fellow. But what if. She stopped... what if he has changed? "No," she said out loud, and she refused to think of that any longer. Finally the time had arrived. As she stepped out the door to the street, she projected elegance. Her selection of rich brown and soft beige fabric radiated grace and charm. Truly a picture of a radiant forty-nine-year-old lady. The doctor was waiting at Doug's door when she arrived.

"I like it," he said.

"What?" she asked.

"Your outfit. It's terrific."

"I hope the Captain in there likes it," she smiled.

"He will, I'm sure he will. I've made arrangements with the staff for the next two hours and we will have no interruptions. I spoke with the psychiatrist and they tell me they have had many discussions with Doug and he continues to grasp more and more of the perplexities of arriving in a strange world. His recovery to this point is remarkable. I'm going in now, and I promise I'll be but a few minutes this time. I'll introduce him to your name and see what his reaction is."

"Okay, Doctor. Please hurry."

As he stepped into Doug's room he found him sitting in a chair, reading a newspaper. He looked up and said, "Doctor Madison, how will I ever catch up with this world?"

"Think of it this way, Captain, you won't be like the rest of us, you won't have time to get bored. Every day will bring some new experiences for you. I wish the remainder of my life would be as exciting and interesting as yours will be."

"Maybe you're right, Doctor, but believe me, it's pretty confusing when there are so many words, phrases and technology that you've never heard. I'm not even sure I can carry on a normal conversation."

"Well, suppose we give you a little test," the Doctor said. "Do you remember a young lady by the name of Lowie Meese?"

At the sound of her name Doug smiled. "Of course I do. That was a long time ago, and besides, how the hell did you find out about her?"

"If we could find her, would you be afraid to talk with her?"

"Now if there's one person in this world I could be at ease with, that's the one it would be. We had a short romance, but it was one that no amount of time could destroy. You clear it with her husband and I'll do the rest."

"I've already made all the arrangements," the doctor answered. "She's right outside the door."

"Are you kidding Doctor?" The doctor shook his head to say "no".

"Well now, I'm not so sure I can handle this. After all, they tell me I've been living with a short-circuited brain for thirty years."

"Just relax, Captain, you'll see everything will fall into place. Now come on, don't let that beautiful lady stand out there. I can tell you she's more nervous than you are."

"Okay, I'm ready, but would you let us alone for this meeting?"

"I wouldn't have it any other way, Captain. Good luck and I'll talk to you later." With that, he left the room. The doctor smiled as he walked towards Lowie.

"Well dear, your moment has arrived. Go into that room and pick up the pieces of what was once your life."

"Thank you, I hope and pray I can do just that." She slowly opened the door and stepped into the room.

The tall man was standing next to a chair. His dark blue eyes sparkled as a bright smile appeared and in a low soft voice he asked, "Lowie Meese? Tell me I'm not dreaming."

"Yes, Doug, it's me, and no, you're not dreaming."

He held out his arms and said, "Dear heart, I still love you."

With that, she ran and fell into his embrace. She could hold back no longer and burst into tears as she said, "Darling I have waited so long to hear you say that. Doug, I love you… love you… love you." They just stood holding each other without saying anything for a long, long time. Finally she whispered, "Darling is it okay for you to be out of bed?"

"Don't worry about me, I'm fine. They may even let me go

home in a few days," and then, as if thinking out loud, he whispered, "wherever home might be."

"Now don't you worry about things like that, your brothers and I will take care of those details."

He slowly stepped back. Still holding her hand, he said, "I can't put it off any longer. I must know, but I'm afraid to ask." He stood there for an agonizing moment looking into her soft tear-filled eyes. "Lowie, are you…" he stopped again.

"What is it, Doug?"

He closed his eyes as he asked, "Are you married?"

"Oh, no, Doug. No, no, no, I'm not married."

"Thank heavens," he said. "Thank you, thank you, thank you," he repeated. "I don't know how I could have taken it if you had said you were." He grabbed her again and held her tight as they both started to laugh.

She spent the next five days at the hospital with Doug. She watched and tried to explain TV. She showed him some of the magazine articles and pictures of jet aircraft; tried to explain atomic energy, space exploration, computers, microwave, lasers; and the list went on and on. They were both so engrossed in his learning process that the days slipped by quickly and each night it became more and more difficult for her to leave him for just a few hours. As she was leaving one night, he pulled her back again, held her very tight for a long time, and then said, "I guess you know when I get out of here, we're going to stop saying all these goodbyes. I think our engagement period has been long enough, don't you?"

She looked up at him and with a smile said, "I don't think anyone could say a thirty-year engagement would be rushing into marriage."

The following morning Doctor Madison came into the room and said, "Well Captain, you can get dressed and get out of here. We're releasing you today."

"You don't have to say that twice, Doctor! I'll be ready in minutes."

"Is someone going to pick you up?" the doctor asked.

"I'll call Lowie," Doug answered. "She said she would do all the driving for a while. I guess she thinks I may be a little rusty in traffic after thirty years on an island with few traffic jams."

It was nearly noon when the doctors and a nurse brought Doug out the front door in a wheelchair. Lowie pulled up to the curb, stopped her car, then hurried to the other side. As she opened the door, she bowed low in front of Doug and with a big grin, said, "You may enter, Captain. You, but not that wheelchair."

Doug stood up, shook hands with everyone, thanking them for all their help and encouragement. "I'm so fortunate to have been under the care of such skilled professionals. I shall always be grateful; and I sincerely mean that."

"We are all grateful," Lowie repeated.

"Okay, you two," Doctor Madison cut in, "suppose you get out of here and start living the good life. I'm sure we'll be reading about you in the papers from time to time."

"I sure hope not," Doug said. "When the newspaper people come, tell them we went on a vacation to the Pacific." He got in the car and closed the door; shook hands again with Doctor Madison and said, "Not only do I have a chauffeur, but I have the prettiest one in town."

"That you do, Captain, that you do."

As they pulled away, everyone was waving goodbye. Doug turned, looked back and waved again. "It's hard saying goodbye to people who have just given you a new world; they have, you know."

"I know," she said, "and I'm so happy I want to shout it to the world."

As she entered the northbound traffic, she said, "Okay, love, just sit back and relax, we're going home."

"That's fine with me, but just where is home?"

"We're going to my place. I live in the Harrisburg area and there won't be any reporters waiting there. I spoke to John on the phone this morning. He said reporters are waiting at his house and there are some at your other brother's home. They don't know about me so we'll not be disturbed there."

"I like that idea, I have a million questions to ask. According to the license plate on that car ahead of us, it really is 1975. It might sound stupid, but I just can't believe it. Something else I can't believe – you not being married." He smiled, "A pretty girl like you? There must have been lots of opportunities."

"I wouldn't say 'lots', but a couple of times. I got so engrossed in the business world, I sort of gave up on the idea; and besides, I kept remembering what you told me… 'I'll be back – some way – somehow – one way or another – I'll be back.' I believed you then and I still do. I did a lot of waiting, a lot of hoping and a great deal of praying, and with God's help, here we are."

He squeezed her hand. "You make me the happiest man in the world."

She smiled. "Let me say it now, for all the years of waiting, what we now have, makes it all worthwhile."

As she continued driving north, she explained how it became possible for her to adopt Robin and how she helped fill a big void in her life. They had talked several times about Robin, but until now she had not explained how the adoption came about.

"I'm a little concerned about meeting my future daughter," Doug said.

"You needn't be, I've told her so much about you through the years, she's anxious to have you back with us. After losing both parents and grandparents in the matter of a few years, her life has had more than its share of grief."

It was late afternoon when they arrived at her apartment. "I guess Robin's not home yet," she said as she unlocked the door.

Suddenly the door flew open; Robin rushed out to Doug and threw her arms around him. "Welcome home, Dad! Welcome home! Come on in. I want you to meet the best grandparents a girl could ever have." Lowie's mother had prepared a big dinner and they spent the next several hours dining and talking, with everyone feeling a little awkward and, at times, a little nervous. As the night wore on, they all became more relaxed and when the hour arrived for her parents to start home, there was a true air of love and understanding.

The next morning after breakfast, Doug suggested they go for a walk. It was a quiet tree-lined street the apartment was on, and as the two walked along holding hands, they approached a bench.

"My dear, will you please have a seat? I have something to ask you."

"But of course, mon Capitan," she teased.

"I want you to know this is the happiest day of my life." After a pause he asked, "We are going to get married, aren't we?"

She smiled and said, "I'll marry you any time, any place; and wherever you go, I'll follow forever."

"Okay, then, it's settled. We'll get married tomorrow."

"We can't do that in this state darling, there's a license and blood test involved and a short waiting period."

"Okay, let's get the license and test right now and I guess after waiting thirty years, we can wait a little longer for the marriage. Besides, I have to check in with someone at the Pentagon. I am still in service, I guess. I know one thing, I need some money. The pay was not very good on that island, but I might have a whale of a paycheck coming from the Air Force! I don't know how they'll handle that." It was as if he were thinking out loud. "You know this is the first time I've thought about my situation. There's a million questions I have to ask somebody; like, how does that plane up there fly without propellers on it?" He looked at her and grinned.

"Dear, I've been here for the last thirty years," Lowie said, "and I still don't know how they fly, but I'm sure in a few days you'll know how to build one."

"Well, you can't imagine how many things are new to me. I heard the doctor talking about a laser beam. Was he serious? That sounds like Buck Rogers to me."

"Honey, don't trouble yourself with things like that, I'm sure the Air Force will want to work with you and brief you on everything."

"I guess you're right, you do realize you're marrying a pretty dumb guy."

"Well I don't care if your IQ is zero, I'll still marry you." They sat and talked for a long time and they decided to find a doctor for the blood test. They learned they would have to wait three days to get married. It would give him time to get squared away with the government.

The next morning he called information at the Pentagon. After briefly explaining his situation, they advised him to call Colonel Broder, which he did immediately. The Colonel asked for his present address and telephone number. He told Doug they would forward a supplementary pay for him and also cut orders for a thirty-day leave. After that, he was to report back to the Pentagon. By that time his service and pay status would be completed. The Colonel told him to relax and enjoy life for a little while. He also assured him a promotion would be waiting when he returned to active service. He turned to Robin and Lowie. "I guess everything's okay so far. They are sending me some money and leave papers for thirty days, by that time they'll know what to do with me."

"We've just been talking about taking you shopping today. There's lots of things you're going to need so we might as well start now."

"Okay, but I'm going to need some help. I feel like a cave man who just woke up in the twentieth century."

The next few days they spent shopping and showing him some of the countless changes that had taken place. The more time they spent with him the more they realized just how difficult it is for someone to step back into modern technology after such a long absence. One day, they went to the International Airport. They drove around trying to get as close as possible to the aircraft. Doug got out of the car, walked over to the fence and watched in amazement at the size and capacity of the planes. He looked at Lowie and smiled, "I wonder if I can talk the Air Force into sending me back to flight school?" She walked over and put her arm around him. "Are you sure you want to do that?" He looked out at the aircraft again and without answering, nodded his head to say "yes."

The next day they made all the arrangements for their upcoming marriage. They planned on a very small and private ceremony hoping not to attract any publicity. So far the news media had not bothered them. Whether it was a courtesy to Doug, or the lack of information as to where he was, they weren't certain. But for whatever reason, they appreciated the privacy. The wedding would be Saturday morning and they would leave immediately after, for a week or two in New England. By this time Doug had received his papers, so now all they were concerned about was having their long-delayed honeymoon together.

The sun rose on a clear bright Saturday morning. By nine thirty, everyone from the two families was seated in the small chapel and what took thirty years of waiting, required but a few moments to complete. Robin had loaded their bags in the car and parked it at the front door. At the conclusion of the ceremony, everyone followed the bride and groom out. The minister put his arms around the two of them and walked to the car. "I'm very happy for you both." He shook Doug's hand and said, "You've been through so many trials and tribulations during the last thirty years, Douglas, I truly hope, and I will certainly pray, that all the bad times are behind you." He then turned to Lowie and took her hand. "My dear lady, you too have endured the long vigil, and now may you reap the rewards. May you two live the best life this world has to offer for more years than we dare hope for."

"Thank you for everything," Doug said, fighting back the tears. "We won't be strangers to your little church when we get back, and to all of you," he continued, "I want to take this moment and say thanks. Thank you all for your understanding, patience and true concern. You've helped me put the pieces back together in my life, and for that, I'll always be grateful. We'll see you all in a few weeks, but for now, it's New England here we come!"

It was about nine o'clock that evening, when they stopped at a motel just a few miles south of Mystic Harbor. It had been a long happy day and now they were alone. With the lights turned low – soft music in the background, they embraced. "Mrs. Douglas Steward, I love you more than life itself."

"Doug, you are my whole world – like the song says, 'I'm glad I waited for you'."

The next morning, the sun rose through dark gray clouds and there was a chill in the air. It was going to be a typical New England autumn day. As they were packing their bags, Lowie paused a moment and said, "Captain Stewart, do you know where your wife would like to visit first?"

He smiled, "Stonington Point?" She nodded her head to say "yes". "You'll have to direct me, I'm not sure I can find it after all these years."

A short time later they were standing with their arms around each other, looking out at the waves rolling in, crashing against the big boulders just below where they stood. They could see a few small fishing boats struggling in the rough sea. The wind was quite cold now. Doug drew his wife closer and softly said, "The cold gray skies of winter all record my love in an endless scroll."

"That's pretty," she said. "What's it from?"

"Oh, a poem I tried to write about this spot a long, long time ago."

"Do you know the rest of it?"

"Afraid not, it's been too long ago."

"All the time you were gone, I never felt so close to you as when Robin and I stood right here as we are now."

"It's a beautiful spot to create memories," he whispered. They spent most of the day sightseeing around Stonington. It was late in the day, as they made their way back to the car.

"It's such a typical, beautiful old New England town," she said. "I think I could stay here forever. Can we come back again sometime?"

"Hopefully, soon and often," Doug said. The days passed quickly as they toured the coastline all the way north to Maine. It was well into the second week before they started south. Nearly three weeks had elapsed before they returned to their home in Pennsylvania.

Chapter Twenty-One

At the end of Doug's leave he called the Pentagon and asked for Colonel Broder. The telephone clicked and then a man answered. "Colonel Broder here."

"Sir, this is Captain Douglas Stewart reporting in."

"Hello Doug, and welcome back." They chatted a few moments and then the Colonel said, "Doug, I have some good news for you. The President wants you to come down to the White House for an official welcome home. How about that, Captain?"

"I don't know Sir. It sounds a little scary, but what the Commander-in-Chief wants, the Commander-in-Chief gets," Doug laughed, "when, and where, do I report?"

"You'll report to my office Monday at 0900 and I'll escort you from here. Everything will be arranged by that time. We'll have your clothing and uniforms ready for you and I'll brief you on what to expect. It'll be fun, Doug; something you'll remember the rest of your life."

"I'm sure it will be Colonel, but I'm not much for the limelight. I know I have little choice, since I'm still in service and he's my Commander."

"Of course, his invitation is for you as well as your lovely bride," Colonel Broder continued. "I'll expect you both at 0900 Monday. If there are any problems, just contact me here at my office."

"Thank you Colonel. We'll be there Monday."

As Doug hung up the receiver he turned to Lowie and said, "Well, Mrs. Stewart, the President of the United States wants to see you."

"Are you serious? Are you going to meet the President?"

"No, we're going to the White House."

"Now I know the President isn't interested in meeting me, but I'm proud he wants to meet my husband."

"Now, that's not the way it is. The Colonel said it's a package deal; besides, I'd be scared to meet him myself."

They were up very early the next morning and immediately started making arrangements for the trip. One of the big concerns for Doug was the publicity that would be surrounding the White House meeting. He wasn't sure he could handle it. He knew he was still a little confused and very much uninformed of all the world changes; especially the technological advances that had taken place while he was confined to his other world – a world no one around him could imagine.

In the afternoon they decided to take a drive to the country. After stopping at a small restaurant for lunch, they drove off the main highway and parked atop a hill overlooking the rolling countryside. They sat there quietly admiring the beautiful view. Finally he said, "I'm sorry I put you through such torment all those years, not knowing if I were dead or alive. Each day I seem to remember and can piece together a little more of those years before that Jap put my lights out, but I have little recollection of the years that followed. Sometimes it nearly drives me nuts. How the hell did I survive if I didn't know what I was doing?"

"The doctors told me you probably did know what to do to survive. Sort of by instinct, they said. With a head injury like you suffered, there is no textbook record. All they really have is theories. They recommended I help you remember our life together before you were injured. So let's give you a little test, and if you fail, you're in big trouble." She opened her handbag and got out a small box. She opened it and said, "Hold out your hand." As he did, she placed the silver wings he had given her on his graduation day into his hand. He smiled, and after looking at them a few moments, held them up and said, "Now these I do remember! Boy! What I went through to get that worthless little piece of silver. I'm really surprised you still have them."

"Don't be silly, you knew I wouldn't let them out of my sight. I can remember that day as if it were yesterday. I was pretty proud of you that day, but I was afraid I'd never see you after you left."

"I think I was in love with you from the first moment I saw you, I acted like some bumbling idiot."

"Well, if I remember that first meeting," she said, "I wasn't exactly the charming sales clerk the boss thought he had hired." They both laughed.

"I guess," Doug went on, "when it comes to idiots, it takes one to know one, but isn't it fun being idiots together?" She leaned over and kissed him. "No way could it be better."

The sun was beginning to set, before they decided to start home. "I guess we must go," she said. "We'll be leaving for Washington first thing in the morning, won't we?" Doug nodded.

"Yeah, I wish I didn't have to go. Meeting Presidents is a little out of my line."

"I guess that's the price you have to pay when you're famous," she teased.

"That's enough. Let's go home," he answered.

When they got home, Robin had already laid out some of the things they would need for the White House visit. "Thank you dear, for taking care of us, but where are your things?"

"I'm not going along. I feel this is your day. This is going to be quite a memorable day and it's you two who deserve the spotlight. There should be only one lady standing by this handsome Captain's side, and that lady has to be my Mom. I'm so happy for you both; so you two go and make some beautiful memories."

It was quite early the next morning when there was a knock at the front door. Doug opened it to find an Air Force Sergeant. "Can I help you?"

"Sir, I have a staff car waiting to take you to Colonel Broder's office at the Pentagon."

"Right, Sergeant, thank you. We'll be ready in a few minutes."

"What is it?" Lowie called.

"The Colonel sent a staff car for us. I guess he thought I don't remember how to drive." After saying goodbye to Robin, they hurried out to the car and in a few minutes, they were out of town and heading south towards Washington. It was a little after nine o'clock when they arrived at the Colonel's office. He was waiting and greeted them warmly. "Doug, we took the liberty of preparing a new uniform for you; complete with your campaign ribbons and wings. We thought it best you be in uniform when you meet the President."

"Thank you Sir, I'm sure you know best in these matters."

"You can change in the room across the hall. It should fit. We had all of the vital statistics on your size."

"If it doesn't, we can always shoot the tailor," he joked. In a few minutes, Doug had changed and the Colonel put in a call for a limousine to take them to the White House. The limousine pulled up to the main entrance.

"Okay, Captain, and Mrs. Stewart, we have arrived."
Lowie smiled.

"Colonel, I'm nervous."

"My dear, that probably makes three of us." They all laughed as they started towards the main entrance.

Once inside, they were escorted to a huge waiting room. Moments after being seated, a lady entered from what appeared to be a concealed door. She smiled and greeted them very warmly. Everyone was treating them as royalty. So much so, Doug was a bit embarrassed. "There will be a few minutes delay before the President can see you," the lady said. "Is there anything I can get you? I'm at your complete service while you are a guest here. So please don't hesitate if you need anything."

"Thank you, ma'am," Doug answered, "but really, there's nothing. We're quite fine."

"My name is Colleen Shultz. I assume you are Mrs. Stewart?" she said, as she shook Lowie's hand.

"Yes, and I'm very happy to meet you, though I must admit, I'm very nervous about meeting the President and all this."

"Please try not to be, my dear. I know the President quite well and he is an absolute joy to be with. I also know he is very anxious to meet you two. Off the record, he told me yesterday, he hoped he wouldn't say something stupid while in your presence." With that, they laughed.

About fifteen minutes later, another door opened and Colonel Broder came in. "Well, if everyone's ready, we'll go in and meet the President now." As they entered the Oval Office, the President was seated at his desk, apparently signing some papers. He looked up immediately, smiling as he rose; then said, "Welcome to our house. I'm both honored and very pleased to meet you." He came across the room, extending his hand, first to Lowie and then to Doug. She was surprised to find him much taller then she imagined. He shook Doug's hand and said, "Welcome home, Captain Stewart. I'm sure I speak for Americans everywhere, when I say we're truly sorry you have lost so much and have been isolated for so long. I hope we can, in some small way, make it up to you. When I first learned of your plight, I wondered how you endured and survived such an ordeal. Doug, I'm truly honored to meet someone of your caliber. Let me say thank you, for all you did for us. I've reviewed you records and, as so many other young Americans, you did an outstanding job under very difficult conditions. Now if you will be so kind, would you mind going out with me to face the news media? I understand there are news people from all over the world out there, but I'll make the ordeal as brief and painless as possible."

"Mr. President, I hope they're not expecting a speech from me," Doug said. He just smiled and answered, "Me either, Doug."

The moment Doug appeared, they were greeted with a barrage of flashbulbs and spectators. The President let it continue for a few moments and then raised both arms and signaled for silence. He stepped to the microphone and with a broad grin, said, "Ladies and Gentlemen, I think at the next news conference, I'll bring Captain Stewart with me, that way, you'll all forget those tough questions you always ask me." There was a roar of laughter. Then he continued. "We have here with us today, not only a man I consider a hero, but a man that has sacrificed a large portion of his life trapped on an enemy-held island for nearly thirty years, and survived most of that time in total isolation. I think, in the truest sense, this is above and beyond the call of duty. Now, in what I am sure is a total surprise to Captain Douglas Stewart, I am authorized to present him with the Congressional Medal of Honor." As he spoke, his aide stepped forward with the box containing the medal. The President took it and placed it around Doug's neck, stepped back and saluted him. Doug was shocked and in complete surprise, for he never once thought his government would be so grateful. He immediately returned his Commander-in-Chief's salute. "Congratulations, Doug," the President said. He again shook Doug's hand. Doug reached out for Lowie's hand, as he moved closer to the mike.

Holding her close to his side, he said in a low voice, "I want to thank the President and the fine people of this great nation. I especially want to thank this beautiful lady, my wife, for never giving up hope. She waited through what must have been more difficult times than what I endured. I shall be forever grateful to her, and I shall never forget the honor I received here today. Thank you." As he stepped back from the mike and embraced her, he gave her a kiss and the huge crowd stood in complete silence. Again, the President thanked them and as his group turned to go back inside, there arose a roar of applause from the crowd.

When they approached the door, Lowie looked up at Doug and said, "I love you, dear heart." He pulled her closer, winked and smiled as they entered the Oval Office again.

"Please be seated," the President said. "Let's chat for a few moments." Everyone sat down. "Now then, Doug, have you had time to think about your future? If you have, I'd be most interested in your plans."

"Mr. President, I have thought, if it is possible, I'd like to continue in the Service for a while."

"I see no problem with that, Doug. As I understand, you are in good physical condition and I'm sure the Air Force could use you."

"I'm sure I'll have to be retrained," Doug said.

"That would be no problem," the President answered. "Uncle Sam's good at that. He does it every day. When you report back to duty, just contact Colonel Broder here and he can get you all squared away."

The Colonel looked at Doug. "How would you like a refresher at Dover Air Force Base? It's close to home and they have everything we'll need right there."

"Sounds good to me, Sir," Doug answered. He looked at Lowie. She smiled and nodded in agreement.

"If everything goes okay in training, at completion there may be a promotion waiting for you," the President said. "After all, we can't hold a man in rank for thirty years without some explanation." Everyone laughed and the President stood up, walked over to Doug, and again shook his hand. "Well, folks, I'm sorry I have to end this very pleasant meeting, but I have to get back to work." He smiled and added, "I work for a pretty tough boss!"

They were escorted out through another area where a limousine was waiting. After everyone was in, Colonel Broder told the driver to return them to his office. As the car pulled away, Colonel Broder looked back at Doug. "Well, what do you think of this day so far, folks?" Doug smiled.

"It's certainly not one we're likely to forget, but I'm glad all of that is over. I still feel very stupid and each day I realize how the world and technology has run away from me. I'm nearly a throwback to the stone age."

Lowie smiled and slapped his hand. "No, you're not from the stone age. You've been home only a little while and already you know more of what's going on in the world than I do, and I never even left the country."

"Captain, don't be too concerned about these things. I'm going to get you set up in a re-educational program and step-by-step, you'll be able to catch up."

"I hope I can handle it, Colonel. I'm really anxious to get started."

A short time later they arrived at Colonel Broder's office. They remained in the car, talking for some time. Finally he said, "Now you folks go on home and relax a week or so and that will give me time to set up your training program. It won't be long before we'll have you up in the wild blue yonder again, Captain."

Doug smiled. "I'm having trouble getting used to the name US Air Force instead of the Army Air Force." He grew silent for a moment and then, as if thinking out loud, said, "I wonder if any of the fellows in my squadron survived? I understand the war went on quite a few months after I went down."

Lowie reached for his hand and held on tight. "That last raid we were on was a hell of a mess." He then grew silent again.

"Doug, I'm sure after the six thirty news tonight, when the country gets a look at who is the latest recipient of the Congressional Medal of Honor, you'll hear from some of those guys," the Colonel said. "It's hard to tell where they might be scattered across the nation, but I'm sure they'll know their squadron leader is finally back home."

"I would really like to know how the other fellows made out; especially Orris, Montgomery, and Bosler. The last time I saw Bosler he was trying to get back to base." Doug paused, then said quietly, "They were good men."

"Well, Doug, you take your wife and go home for a while and when the training program is ready, I'll get word to you and we'll get you back to active duty."

"Sounds good to me, Colonel. Thank you. Thank you for everything."

It was late afternoon when they left Washington, and the conversation from there until they arrived home was all about the day's exciting events. As they pulled into their driveway Doug said, "I hope the men in my squadron receive recognition for all the miseries they went through."

"I hope so too," Lowie said, "but many times great heroes go unnoticed."

It was two weeks later that Doug received orders to report to Dover Air Force Base. The orders were signed by Colonel Broder.

There was a memo with them, in which the Colonel wished him good luck and if there was anything he needed, he was to call his office at the Pentagon. He ended the memo stating, "I'll keep in touch."

On the day he had to leave, Doug told Lowie he was going to get processed and settled into his routine. As soon as he knew what his schedule would be, he would call and let her know. "I don't want you to go," she said as they kissed goodbye, "but I know you have to."

"I promise it won't be as long as the last time," he smiled.

"It better not be," she said. "As the song goes, 'I've grown accustomed to your face'."

"And don't you ever forget it," he laughed. She stood in the doorway and watched as he drove away.

As she walked back into the house, a lot of old memories returned. She remembered, many years ago she stood in the dark of night alone, except for an old man who was the guard of a small gate leading to the airport ramp. She was still waving goodbye, long after the drone of Doug's plane and the flashing marker lights had disappeared. She could still hear the old man softly saying, "Don't cry missy, he'll be back, he'll come back," and he was right. Her man did come back, but the price they both paid was much too high.

It was nearly seven o'clock that evening before Doug was able to call home. He felt like a new recruit. It took most of the day just to get his equipment and orders assigned. The Base Commander called him to Headquarters and talked at length about the training cycle they had assigned him to. It was obvious the Air Force wanted him as badly as he wanted to serve. "We need your experience," the Commander said. "After we get your qualifications upgraded, I'm sure, with your combat experience, you'll be able to contribute a great deal to the Air Force. We need combat flight instructors, and I think you'll make a good one."

When he called home he told Lowie it was like a pep rally. "But it made me feel good. I don't know if the Base Commander was serious or not, but I'm going to try like hell to catch up to this world."

"Well, Honey, I'm sure the Commander meant every word, and I agree with him. You have a great deal to contribute to the Air Force. The only thing I don't like about it is we will be apart from time to time."

There was a pause on the other end of the line. "But it's not like the war. As soon as I get through with this, I'll be assigned and it'll be like a regular job."

"I know," she said, "and remember, I'm with you in whatever you want to do."

"I better hang up now. Tomorrow's another big day, but I'll be home this weekend."

"Be very careful and hurry back," Lowie said.

The weeks passed and Doug was able to go home every weekend. They would go out to dinner or maybe just take a drive. Sometimes, they would park and talk for hours. She could see Doug advancing both in worldly events and in technology. He felt like a kid in a candy store, he told her. Everything was so new and he was really impressed with how fast and powerful these new planes were. As they talked, she knew they had made the right decision for him to stay in service. He was now a really happy man.

He was halfway through the training cycle when he called Lowie and asked her to come down to the base for the weekend. He wanted her to see the type of aircraft he was learning to fly. He suggested she arrange her travel time about three o'clock in the afternoon, Friday. He told her to ask the M.P. at the gate for directions to the parking area for flight line 32 and he would meet her there.

The next Friday, she arrived a little early and walked from the parking area over to the high fence, and watched the aircraft landing and taking off. There was a lot of noise and activity and then, suddenly, one of the planes turned and started to taxi across the tarmac towards her. It stopped just beyond the fence. She saw Doug waving to her, as he shut the jet engine down. The ground crewman attached the ladder for Doug to climb down. After taking his helmet off, he hurried over to her, as he pointed back, laughing, he called, "How do you like the big bird?"

"It's much too noisy for me," she yelled.

"I'll be right with you. I have to get the guard to let me out the gate." A few minutes later, they were standing with their arms around each other, watching some of the other planes coming in. "If I would have had an aircraft like that in the Pacific, I think I could have won the war single-handed. They are so superior to anything we had then, it boggles the mind. Although they are the ultimate in a fighting machine, they lack something our P-38s had. I guess it's character. These just don't have character. I miss that drone of those P-38 engines. It's funny, when I fire them up, I still expect to hear that same roar, and the jet just sits there and whines."

"Well, Honey, I guess that's the price of progress," she said.

He stood there a few moments without answering, and then as if thinking out loud, said, "Yeah, I guess you're right. That's one of the prices we pay."

They drove to the other side of the base where the coffee shop was located, and spent nearly two hours talking. He was explaining how the training was intensifying. He joked about feeling like a father to all the other fellows in the training cycle. Everyone was treating him very well and sometimes his instructors were reluctant to correct him when he made a mistake; partly out of respect and partly because they were intimidated by his age and experience. He asked them individually and collectively to please forget what the news media stated about him and just teach him what he had to learn. She reached across the table to hold his hand; smiled, and said, "Douglas Stewart. My humble hero!" Then they both laughed.

They spent the rest of the weekend together and Monday morning found them separated again. For the next several months they were only able to spend the weekends together. When Doug had finished his training cycle, he was immediately assigned as a Flight Instructor to the Flight Training Staff. A few weeks later, they both decided it would be better to rent an apartment and move closer to the base. This decision, they agreed, was the right one.

Chapter Twenty-Two

It was nearly three months later when early one evening the telephone rang. Lowie answered and was told it was a long distance, person-to-person call for Douglas Stewart. She handed him the phone. "It's for you, long distance."

"Yes operator, this is Douglas Stewart."

There was a short silence and then a man said, "Hello Doug. This is a call from out of your past history. I flew as your wingman for a while. I saw you on TV with the President and I just wanted to add my congratulations and to welcome you back home. I'm former Lieutenant Bosler. You may not remember me but I just wanted to let you know, some of the old squadron survived, and I, for one, never forgot you. After seeing you again on TV, it made me feel proud to have served with you."

Doug cut in, "Bosler! I can't believe it! I don't know how you survived that mess over there, but I'm sure glad you did, and you know as well as I do, I don't really deserve the medal the President gave me. If anyone of us did, I'm sure it was you, and if you didn't get a chest full of medals, you should have!" Doug said. "Where are you living now?"

"I'm back at my home in Idaho. I thought maybe we could get together sometime."

"That's a great idea. When can you make it in? The Air Force has me tied up right now for a while; but we would sure like to have you come back East to see us as soon as possible."

"I have another reason for wanting to talk to you, Doug. I feel it's pretty important."

"Just give us the word when you can make it back and we'll pick you up at the airport." They talked a few more minutes and Bosler told him he would try for the following weekend. After hanging up the phone, Doug told his wife all about Bosler. "He really seemed troubled, so I invited him in for a visit. Apparently, he wants to talk to me about something very important."

"How soon can he get in this way?" she asked.

"He told me he was going to try for next weekend. Whatever it is that's troubling him, it must be important."

Later that week, Doug had just returned to base, after a training mission with a student, when a call came through to report to the Base Commander's office. On his way to headquarters, he couldn't help but wonder what this was all about. As he entered the office, the Commander looked up from his desk. Doug stepped forward and stood at attention. As the General stood up, he saluted him. "At ease, Captain. I called you in to give you some good news and to extend my congratulations. A long-overdue promotion has come through for you. I received the orders from the Pentagon this morning. You're now a full Colonel, Doug! Again, congratulations."

"Thank you, Sir. This is considerably more than I expected."

"You deserve those silver eagles, Doug, and I'm pleased to be able to present them to you. I also want to take this time to tell you, I'm getting some fine reports on your work with our advanced students. We all knew you could contribute to our program, but we didn't fully realize how much. Thanks again."

It was only a few minutes later, when Doug was on the phone calling Lowie. "I have some good news, I just got promoted today."

"Let me guess," she teased. "You're now Major Stewart." He was silent for a few seconds and then said, "No."

"You mean you got Lieutenant Colonel?"

"Try full Colonel," he answered.

"Wow! That's fantastic! I'm so very happy for you. Can we go out and celebrate tonight?"

"You bet we can. I'll be home as soon as possible."

"Colonel Stewart," she said. She then repeated it. "That has a nice ring to it. I like that."

"That's enough of that," Doug laughed. "I'll be home soon."

About two weeks later, as Lowie was unloading the groceries from the station wagon, the telephone rang. As she answered it, she heard a man saying, "Hello, Mrs. Stewart? This is Bosler. I was in Doug's squadron during the war. I'm at the airport now. If you can give me directions, I'll drop by your place and take you and Doug out to dinner someplace tonight."

"You'll do no such thing," she said. "You tell me how to recognize you and I'll pick up you and your luggage there at the airport."

"Well, okay, if you think it's all right with Doug."

"I'm very sure; in fact, he's been looking forward to your arrival since the night you called."

"Okay, then. When you get here I'll be standing close to the main entrance. I'm wearing a blue blazer and my luggage has a big 'USA' sticker on it."

"Very good. I'll be there in about twenty minutes."

She had no problem spotting him on her arrival. They chatted a few moments and then she drove by the base at Dover on their way home. "This is where Doug is flying out of, now," she explained. "He's a combat Flight Instructor and he's having a great time at it."

"It's going to be fun just talking about the old days we shared," Bosler said. "It was pretty rough some times; but you know, after all these years…" he stopped, and there was a silence for a few moments. "…you know… I still miss it. It sounds crazy, but it's true."

"I can understand that," she said.

"Those were exciting times and we were all young then." Bosler smiled, "Sometimes I get bored with my life; but then I see young people standing around on street corners, doing nothing, it's disgusting. I think to myself, what memories could they possibly share and talk about when they get old? They're doing nothing but wasting their lives." She nodded in agreement. It was nearly four o'clock when they arrived home and she immediately started the evening meal. Doug would be home about five thirty. She noticed Bosler seemed a little nervous about meeting him after all these years. Several times, he started to tell her something, but each time he changed the subject. She sensed he was very disturbed about something.

Finally a car stopped in front of the house. It was a young Lieutenant who lived in the next block. He and Doug shared rides to the base.

A moment later Lowie greeted him at the front door. "I have a surprise for you." She smiled. "I picked up one of your old buddies at the airport, a while ago."

As they were talking, Bosler came to the door. He and Doug just stood and looked at each other a moment and then Doug grabbed the hand of his old friend. He put his arm around his shoulder and said, "Welcome to our house, Mr. Bosler. You can't imagine how glad I am to see you again. After our last raid together

– when I was going down – I wasn't sure I'd ever see any of you guys again."

"Well Doug, it's been a lot of years, but here we are again. I couldn't believe it when I saw you on TV. I told my wife, that man standing there with the President was once my Wing Commander. It must be thirty years since I saw him last, and there he is, on TV! By the way, congratulations on receiving the CMH. You sure deserved it."

"Come on, Bosler. I didn't do anything a million other guys didn't do."

"Sure you did and you did it better. And I know you're the only American ever engaged in the thirty-some-odd-year-war," he joked. "I'll always remember the day we lost radio contact on our way back to the base. That's one reason I'm here now."

"What do you mean?"

"Oh, it's a long story. Let's wait 'till after dinner."

The next two hours were spent talking about old times; some happy, some not so. As the conversation came around to Doug's plane becoming disabled, Bosler asked, "Do you really know what happened?"

"Oh, I think so," Doug answered with a smile.

"You do know that it was one of our planes that got you? You remember, you sent me up to a higher altitude because of an engine problem, while you stayed at our planned altitude to draw any fire we might encounter on the way back to base. While I had the best seat in the house," Bosler continued, "I saw the whole rotten scene. What I witnessed, I kept to myself all these years and it's been eating at me ever since. When I saw you on TV, I knew I had to talk to you about it. Tell me, do you know who shot you down?" There was a long silence. Doug looked across the room at Lowie. She immediately saw the hurt in his dark blue eyes. A look she knew all too well, but hadn't seen for a long time now.

"Can we change the subject?" she cut in.

"No, it's okay," Doug said. "I guess we better get it out in the open. I thought it was going to happen some time. I'll let Bosler tell what he thinks happened."

"Well, let me give a little background to this story. The outfit Doug and I were in at that time was small and from time to time we would get new men to replace our casualties. One time they sent us a certain Lieutenant Zimm. His Dad was a US Senator, and it wasn't long 'till we all had him figured out. His sole purpose was to pick up some service background for his political future, and he didn't care who got hurt along the way. He was a lousy pilot and a miserable person to deal with. There was one thing he was good at. As soon as the combat flying action started, he could always find a way to run with his plane and hide. It got so, that on every mission, we could hear Doug calling for him to stay close; but every mission, it was the same thing over again. The louse would fly away and hide, leaving us holding the bag. The last mission Doug and I flew together, he did the same thing; but this time, it was a lot bigger operation than what we were used to. The mission was so long we had a real fuel problem. We had to stay on course, and fly straight lines or not make it back at all. Lieutenant Zimm flew as usual. As soon as the Japs were spotted, he disappeared. None of us saw him again for about half-an-hour. I was close to Doug in another plane that had made it through the raid. We were shot up pretty bad and on our way back to our base, that other plane must have ditched in the ocean because I never saw him again. It was a few minutes after that one went down, when I started having all kinds of trouble with my plane. That's when Doug told me to climb as high as I could and he would stay on our assigned course, to draw the fire if we ran into any stray Japs on our way back. That way I might make it back to our base. For a while it looked real good for me, but not so good for Doug. Thanks in part to that worthless creep, Lieutenant Zimm."

"Why?" Lowie asked. "What did he do?"

He looked at her for a moment without answering. Then said, "Zimm shot Doug down!" There was a long silence. She looked first at Doug and then back at Bosler.

"But how? Why?"

"Doug was having trouble keeping his plane in the air. I heard him say his engines were overheating. Zimm must have been close enough to hear that, too. He dropped down on Doug through the cloud layer and opened fire. What he didn't know was that I, too, was in the area. That he didn't know because Doug had sent me so much higher than our original planned flight."

"But why would he want to shoot Doug?"

"I told you, he wanted to be a hero when he got back to Washington, and Doug knew too much. Zimm knew he had to get rid of him, and from that moment until now, it has worked, but I'll be damned if he's going to get away with it any longer."

She looked at Doug. "Did you know this is what happened?"

"Yeah – I saw enough of his plane to know who it was, but who was I to tell? I'm sure the Japs that put me in a cage wouldn't have been too interested at that time. I was mad as hell, but later I just thought, *oh, well, nobody would believe me anyway.* So I put it out of my mind."

"Well, Doug, that's the main reason I knew I had to talk to you. I don't know how politically minded you are, or if you have had time to catch up on the political picture, but I can tell you…" he paused a moment as he looked at Doug, and then at Lowie. "…the Senator Zimm we now have in Washington is the one and the same."

Lowie put her hand to her mouth in disbelief. "Dear God in heaven – no," she cried, "he's one of our presidential candidates and he's expected to win!" She went over and put her arm around Doug. "Honey, what are we going to do? You can't let a horrible man like that become President!"

"Whatever you decide," Bosler said, "I'll be with you one hundred percent of the way. You can count on that. I'm the only person in the world that saw the whole crummy scene, and I'm for nailing that bastard to the wall. You sleep on it tonight Doug, and let me know in the morning. Whatever you decide, you know I'll honor that decision."

Doug just nodded his head in agreement. "I just wish this guy had never entered my life. He's been nothing but grief to me from day one of our meeting. Now here he is again. Do you two know what kind of a mess this will cause? This could be a political bombshell! I don't know Bosler, I don't know if we should cause a stink like that or not. Like you say, we better sleep on this one; maybe things will look different in the morning."

"Okay, Doug, try to get some sleep and thanks again for letting me spend the weekend with you."

"We're glad to have you," Lowie said. "We're happy to have you spend some time with us." By now it was getting late and everyone agreed it was time to get some sleep.

The next morning they had breakfast about nine o'clock and then Doug suggested they go for a drive in the country. After driving a while, Doug crossed a small bridge and pulled over close to the stream. There was a picnic table nearby. "Okay," he said, "everybody out. Let's go over to the table and do some serious talking." He sat down with Lowie at his side. She reached out and held his hand.

"Well Bosler, I've made a decision. I guess you're right. This guy Zimm would be a disaster in the White House."

"Then you'll help me expose him?" Bosler asked.

Doug nodded his head to say "yes".

"You're doing the right thing," Lowie said.

"Well I hope so." He paused a moment. "I just hope none of us gets hurt through this. Do you have any plan as to how this should be done?" he asked.

"Well, if you want me to, I'll call a news conference and make the announcement. That's all it will take. From there, we'll just play it by the ear."

Doug shut his eyes. "Can you see those headlines? Boy, is this ever going to raise hell in the political arena. I hope you two are ready for a lot of harassment because this is going to explode like a bomb. We're right in the middle, and once started, there's no turning back."

"We're in it together, right to the end," Lowie said, "and I know it's the right thing to do."

"Well, Bosler, when do we drop the shoe – tomorrow?"

"No, I think we better go back home and line up our attorneys first. I'm leaving on the six o'clock flight today. When everything's ready, I'll call you."

"Well, if you're leaving at six, I guess we better start home," Doug said.

On the way back home, Doug said, "By the way Bosler, I never did ask you, did you make it back to base that same day?"

"Hell no! My engines went dead and I had to ditch in the ocean. When I leveled out to put it in the drink, I spotted a ship off to my left. I thought, *Whoopee! How lucky can I be?* I stretched my glide a bit and just as I started to flair out for a landing close to the ship, I spotted the flag. Hell, it was a Jap ship!"

"Now there's real luck!" Doug joked. "What happened? How did you survive?"

"Not very well, I'm sorry to say. I thought they would shoot me as soon as I got out of the plane but they hauled me on board and interrogated me for two days with their special system, which I don't think I'll discuss right now. Then they threw me down the hold where there were a bunch of other prisoners. They looked more like skeletons than men. Most of them never survived. I ended up in a work camp in Japan. I didn't know the war was over until some GIs came in the gates one day. A few weeks later I was in a hospital at Seattle. It took six months to get well enough to go home and I ain't never going back!"

"Holy Hell!" Doug said. "Can't say as I blame you. Here all along I thought you made it back to base that same day."

"Well you don't know how often I wished I had," Bosler said.

Bosler looked at Lowie. "Do you object to war stories, especially if they are not pleasant?"

"No. After all, I'm from a military family, and let's face it, our histories can't be changed."

"Well, Doug," he continued, "the Japs took me to a POW camp. I never did know where it was located and after I got back, I really didn't give a damn. There were a lot of Aussies held there. Some of them were like walking skeletons. Those Jap guards were brutal. Those first few weeks I was there, I didn't get enough food to keep an ant alive. That was their way of keeping the prisoners under control; starve everyone to near death. Then when they had you in that condition, the little bastards took delight in torture and beatings, which never stopped. They especially hated pilots. I was in a cage with an Aussie pilot who had been shot down six months before they got me. You can imagine what shape he was in. He was so thin and had so many cuts and welts over his body, it made me sick to my stomach just to see his condition. We talked as much as we could about everything, just to keep from going mad. He told me about his life before the war and how he decided to be a pilot. He had a girlfriend back in Australia and he was just trying to survive to get back to her. We talked about her every day and sometimes we would have to cry. It got so I felt she was also a friend of mine. I promised if we survived, I'd come to their wedding. They lived just outside Hobart. He had been a big fellow. He was about 6'3" which made it even worse for him because the Japs hated anyone who was big and tall.

"One day there was a lot of shouting and screaming outside. Some guards came in and dragged us both out. There were about forty soldiers, standing in a big circle, shouting and waving their rifles in the air. They made my friend walk out to the center of the crowd. As they all laughed, the officers started beating him and spitting on him. Finally they made him kneel down as one of them raised his saber and held it there for a long time. The men jumped around, laughing and shouting. I stood there in horror, as the man with the saber brought it down with both hands! My friend's head fell to the dirt as his body lurched backwards. I had never seen anything so horrible in my life and those dirty bastards made a celebration out of this inhuman act! And I'm not supposed to be bitter! I'll never forget – nor forgive – those bastards!"

Again he looked at Lowie. "I'm sorry. I just had to tell someone about that horrible act. I'm sure it was not an isolated incident, but it's something I've lived with to this day and never told anyone. Again, I'm sorry to have unloaded it on you."

"No need to be sorry," Doug cut in. "Like Lowie said, 'we can't escape from history.'"

Chapter Twenty-Three

Three days later, Bosler called to tell them he had retained an attorney. It was now up to Doug. There was a long pause and then Doug said, "I know how strong you and Lowie are on this matter, and I agree Zimm should be stopped. I just wish there was some other way, but I guess there isn't; so... okay... call your news people and see if anyone is interested."

"You're doing the right thing," he told Doug, "and don't worry – all we're doing is telling the truth."

The next morning the story hit all the headlines and Doug was summoned to base headquarters. He entered the Base Commander's office and was met by the Joint Staff. "It seems you're in the middle of a hell of a controversy. My phone has been ringing since early this morning. Some of the calls have been from Senator Zimm's office, and believe me, they are really hostile."

"I'm sure they are," Doug said. "But this wasn't exactly all my idea. You see, there is a witness to a crime and that witness has been waiting all these years to reveal the truth. He just asked me for that opportunity and I said okay – go for it – so there's no turning back now, and if it means the end of my career, Commander, so be it."

"Now hold on Colonel Stewart; no one's going to end your career. We just want to hear the story and we want to hear it from you. Some of the things I've been reading this morning, if true, are going to blow the lid off Washington. Senator Zimm is odds-on favorite to be our next president. To be charged with less-than-truthful hero status and on top of all that – attempted murder – well, I can assure you the sparks are going to fly. Now tell us, just what did happen?"

Doug pointed to a chair. "May I?"

"Of course, Colonel. Please be seated."

"Well I guess I'll start at the time Lieutenant Zimm entered our outfit. At first the fellows in our squadron, as well as myself, just thought the new Lieutenant was some 'hot shot' who would be with us a few weeks and then, without explanation, be shipped back to the States. You know how that little political game works." The Base Commander nodded in agreement. "Well, every day he was with us, he became more obnoxious. You just couldn't reason with him. Every mission we flew he made sure he stayed out of danger, at the expense of us all. He disliked me even more intensely than the rest because at the time, I was the squadron leader. On the last mission I flew, we got shot up pretty bad. But Lieutenant Zimm pulled the same old trick; he just flew away and waited. I was helping Lieutenant Bosler get back to base. He had a very sick aircraft. The rest of the fellows that had made it through the raid were ahead of us on their way back to the base. We all were very low on fuel, but without any deviation in our course back, we could make it. I had told Lieutenant Bosler to climb as high as he could and I would remain at our original flight-plan altitude. If we did encounter any Jap planes on the way back, they would in all probability, be at the lower altitude. Everything was going along okay when suddenly I caught sight of one of our P-38s. It was just a little to the rear and at four o'clock position. When I looked back again I saw some yellow flashes coming out of the guns. I said to myself out loud, 'the son of a bitch is trying to shoot me down.' I knew I was a sitting duck. My engines were running too hot, so there wasn't much for me to do but try to lose him in a cloud layer below us. So I dove. As I did, I was taking some direct hits. One must have gotten an oil line because the pressure fell to nearly nothing. The last time I saw him, there was no mistaking those red bars painted on the tail vertical stabilizers, I knew it was Lieutenant Zimm. Lieutenant Bosler was right there, sitting high above us and he saw the whole damn circus. After waiting all these years, he came to visit me recently and begged me to let him go public with this. I gave it a lot of serious thought and finally agreed. So that brings us to this point. Whatever might happen from here, Commander, I don't know."

There was a long silence in the room. "You are aware that Senator Zimm is running for the Presidency," one officer said, "and is expected to win. My question is, as I'm sure a lot of other Americans will be, is this some kind of a high-powered political mud-slinging?"

Doug stood up. He was visibly angered. "In answer to your question, Major, I haven't been back in civilization long enough to know a damn thing about politics. All I know is what happened to me over there cost me thirty years of my life, and if the disclosure of that incident disrupts someone's political aspirations, I'd say the penalty for the act has been at a bargain-basement price tag."

"Gentlemen, gentlemen," the commander cut in, "that's not what this meeting is for. I asked Colonel Stewart to come here to tell us what's behind the headlines in this morning's paper. We now know, and Colonel, I want to thank you for doing just that. Now, gentlemen, I suggest we all get back to our duties."

Doug was the first to leave the office and went directly to the classroom where the students were waiting.

When he arrived home that evening, Lowie met him at the front door. "And what kind of a day did you have?" she asked with a smile.

"Well, all I can say, it was different." He told her of the meeting at the Base Commander's office to start the day and from there, it got progressively worse.

"Well, it wasn't much better here, either. I stayed indoors all day. There must have been a dozen news reporters around this area. I turned the TV on, and then I knew why. Apparently no one has been able to interview Senator Zimm yet, and it's driving the news people nuts."

Doug just smiled. "Oh, he's lining up an army of lawyers, you can bet on that."

"Are you going to get legal help?"

"Well, not just yet. I'm sure there will be some kind of Senate hearing, or whatever they do in cases like this."

"Honey," she interrupted, "there has never been a case like this before. Here's a man that is just about to move into the White House and is going to be charged with conspiracy, attempted murder, and heaven knows what else."

Doug smiled again. "I'm going to answer all their questions truthfully. They can't shoot me for that."

After dinner, they turned the TV on and watched the news and some special programs that were devoted to the widely expanding controversy. "I better call Bosler," Doug said. "I bet he's getting some real heat by now." A few minutes later he was talking to his friend, and as he guessed, things were beginning to happen. But he was well prepared. He and his lawyer had covered all the possibilities. And yes, he was preparing to come back East. He was already told he would be spending some time in Washington. Doug immediately suggested he stay at their home. It would be best all around.

The next morning as Doug was leaving to go to the base, he was met with a big gathering of news reporters, most of whom were shouting the same type of questions. "Is it true you have always disliked Senator Zimm because of his political power?" "Are you planning to enter politics?" "Do you know Senator Zimm has denied all charges, and is going to make a national broadcast tonight?"

Doug kept repeating "No comment" as he hurried to the car. He waved back to his wife who was standing at a window watching him as he backed out of the driveway.

Once on base, he went about his duties without any more harassment. About noontime, he called home and asked if the reporters had given up and left. She said they had and Bosler called to let them know he would be coming in on the nine o'clock flight tonight. Also, Colonel Broder called from the Pentagon, and left a message for him to return his call as soon as he got home. "What's up?" Doug asked. "Did he sound upset?"

"No. In fact, he made it clear he was on your side."

"Boy, I'll soon need a score card to know who is for and who is against me," Doug joked.

It was late that evening when the phone rang again. Lowie listened a moment and then handed it to Doug. "It's for you."

When he answered, a man asked, "Is this Colonel Douglas Stewart?"

"Yes it is. Can I help you?"

There was a long silence and the man said, "About this matter in the news concerning you and Senator Zimm, you really don't expect people to believe this fairy tale, do you?"

"I don't care who may or may not believe me. Some friends of mine, as well as myself, feel it's something the voters should know, and after they have the facts they can make their own decisions."

"You must realize, Colonel, there's no way you can prove these accusations, so why don't you save yourself, as well as everyone else, all the grief that's sure to come? Think of it this way, Doug. There could very well be a promotion coming your way before you retire, and a General's retirement is always better than a Colonel's."

"Well, I can't argue with that, mister, but I consider myself just an aircraft jockey. Hardly the qualifications for a General."

"No, I guess we'll just let happen whatever happens."

"Thanks for calling, but I'm not interested." With that, Doug hung up the phone. He looked at his wife. "I believe I've just been offered a bribe to drop this whole issue, and whoever that fellow was, he seemed to have a lot to offer."

"Honey, I'm starting to get scared," she said.

"Now don't worry about anything. They'll call Bosler and me before committee. We'll tell them what happened. And they'll do whatever they want, and that will be the end of it."

"I hope you're right," she said, "but I'm getting a little scared."

That night, Bosler arrived on schedule. When they got back to Doug's home the three sat and talked for several hours. Bosler told them what had happened on his end so far; including the fact that he, too, was offered a bribe to drop everything.

The next morning, Bosler went to Washington to meet with an attorney his lawyer back home had lined up for him to work with when the time came. Doug, as usual, reported to the flight school. When he arrived there was a message waiting for him simply stating, "Report to General Ginter's office at base headquarters." He went immediately to meet the Commander. This time there was no one else in the office. The General asked him to sit down. "Colonel, I've been instructed to release you from duty. You are to report to the Pentagon tomorrow. It seems Senator Zimm is questioning your sanity."

"I can believe that, General. I guess before this is over, he'll be trying a lot of things."

"Well anyway," the General continued, "you are to first report to a Colonel Broder, and he is going to take you to the Justice Department. There's going to be a Senate subcommittee hearing on the matter. I wouldn't care to trade places with you for the next two weeks."

"Sir, I'm not exactly looking forward to it myself."

"Well, as of now, you're off duty. Good luck. And I hope you get this matter resolved quickly. I need you here at this base; not at the Pentagon."

"Thank you, Sir. I'm sorry if I caused you any inconvenience."

Doug left the office and walked slowly back to his car. He got in and just sat there for a long time, thinking of all the things that had happened in the last several weeks. He shook his head as if not believing it. Finally, he started the car and drove out of the main gate and started home. It was about ten o'clock when he arrived. As he pulled into the driveway, Lowie heard the car and came out to meet him.

"Why are you back already?" she called. "Is anything wrong?"

"No, not really," he said as he got out of the car and started towards her. Just as he met her there was a loud cracking noise behind him. Lowie screamed, "What was that?"

"Gunfire!" he yelled as he grabbed her arm and pulled her to the ground – but not before there was another burst. She screamed again and, as she fell to the ground, Doug threw himself on top of her. Blood was now splattered over her face and started to run down her arm. He tried to drag her under the car, but he collapsed, still holding her down on the driveway. As he blacked out, blood was streaming down the side of his body, and there were several wounds on his left arm and shoulder. He had been hit from the rear! At that instant there was a loud noise from across the street as a black van, with its tires spinning and the engine screaming, sped away from the curb and down the street. By now, several neighbors came running out. One man took a quick look and ran to call the ambulance and police. Both victims were lying on the ground unconscious and were losing a great deal of blood. What seemed like hours was but minutes, until the ambulance was on the scene. The men quickly loaded them into the ambulance, and with sirens wailing, sped away towards the hospital. The police were trying to piece together the story of just what had happened. At the hospital, there was near panic as a team of doctors tried to stem the flow of blood from the two victims. It would take hours before they would have any success at repairing the many wounds; and several days before there would be any hope of the survival of either.

A week passed. The FBI had now entered the case. Doug was still listed as very critical and Lowie remained in a coma. She had suffered a head wound and a bullet wound in her lower arm. At least two bullets had hit Doug. The most serious had entered his back and came through his left shoulder. Lowie had been hit from the right side of her head, but the bullet did not penetrate. It had caused a massive skull fracture. The Pentagon had ordered a security watch around the clock. No one was to enter either room without authorization. The government had tried to suppress all information on the incident. But little by little, the news leaked out and soon all the papers, TV and radio stations were consumed with the story. There was an "all-points" bulletin put out for the recovery of the vehicle suspected of being used in the murder attempt. The authorities knew logic would dictate their first suspects would have to include Senator Zimm. The Senator, meanwhile, had already anticipated this conclusion. He therefore requested and received permission to make a national TV appearance, disavowing any knowledge or connection with the attempted assassination plot. The Justice Department had ordered that as soon as Colonel Stewart's condition would permit, he be removed from the hospital he was now in, and be transferred to an undisclosed location where his security could be ascertained. A few days later, this was accomplished. When it was questioned whether or not Mrs. Stewart's life was also in jeopardy, the agency deemed not. Special agent Myles Barkley was put in total command of the security and safety of the chief witness for the upcoming senate investigating hearings. The transfer was conducted by night and Doug had little knowledge of most of the actions.

It was nearly two weeks, before he was completely out of danger and recovering well. As for his wife, she still remained in a coma. Doug was kept fully informed of her condition on a regular basis. He was also informed the location of his new home for the next few weeks. It was Bar Harbor, Maine. He would remain here in the secure isolation, or until his protection for the upcoming Senate hearings could be guaranteed.

It was very early on a Saturday morning, when the total reality of all that had happened in the last two weeks came crashing down on him. "Who's in charge here?" he demanded.

"I am, Colonel," said a man entering the room. "I'm James C Wesley and I've been put in charge of the team whose job it is to protect you twenty-four hours a day, and we intend to do just that."

"Well, Mr. Wesley…"

"Please, Colonel, just call me 'J C'. Everyone does."

"Well all right, J C, I have some damn important questions to ask someone. So, I guess it might as well be you. First, I want some straight answers… such as… exactly what condition is my wife in? Hell, I don't know for sure if she even survived the attack."

"I can assure you Sir," J C cut in, "your wife, like you, was hit, but she is recovering, and just as soon as she is able to be moved, she will probably be transferred to this facility so the two of you can be together. That's how Mr. Myles Barkley wants it, and that's how it will be."

"The next thing is," Doug asked, "have they uncovered anything in an investigation?"

"Yes, they have. At first they didn't know if whoever shot at you was just some crazy nut wanting publicity, or if it was a conspiracy to keep you from testifying. They have found the van that was used. Of course, it had been stolen, but they are going over it piece-by-piece, looking for clues. So far, they have determined there were at least two men in it at the time of the shooting. Also, your friend Bosler was put under protective custody, just in case they try another strike. From what they have put together so far, they're positive the people in the van were professionally paid killers. Apparently, the assassination plan was unexpectedly disrupted when your wife came out of the house to meet you. This forced them to open fire while you were too close to your car. They weren't expecting anyone else on the scene at that particular time. The plan must have been to get you as soon as you cleared the car, and before you reached your front door."

"If my wife dies, I'll spend the rest of my life hunting those bastards down."

"I know how you feel, Colonel, I'd feel the same way, but don't worry, we'll get them."

Another week passed and the security officers kept assuring him that his wife was recuperating well. They felt that any day now, she would make a full recovery. The following day, his doctors permitted him to take his first walk down to the beach. The path wound its way down between and around the big boulders that formed the rugged coastline for miles in each direction. The wind blowing in from the sea was quite cool. He sat down on a big boulder, leaned back, and gazed out over the sea, as the gulls chattered in excitement because of his presence. His thoughts raced back through the many years to another time and place. A moment in his life he had shared with his love, Lowie. That moment was to change his life forever. "I love you, Lowie," he said out loud as he covered his face with his hands. "Please don't leave me now. I love you more than ever."

"We better go back now, Colonel," one of the security officers called down. He waved his hand in acknowledgment; slowly got to his feet and started back.

The next day he returned to the same area. This time he brought with him a pen and notebook. He sat down and leaned back, watching the waves roll in. They crashed against the rocks just below him. After sitting there a few minutes, he started to write:

> I stand alone on the windswept shore,
> A lone seagull soars high above.
> I hear its fading but distinct call;
> It's just as I, alone with love.
>
> The restless pounding, roaring surf,
> Those golden oaks on a distant knoll,
> The cold, gray skies of winter,
> All record my love in an endless scroll.
>
> As the red and gold of autumn
> With the wild winds beckoning call,
> My heart reflects your haunting image
> So strong, even the winds will be stilled in awe.
>
> Just as the tears still cloud my eyes,
> Just as our star above still shines,
> I ask the fleeting wind again
> Are you my love? Are you still mine?
>
> If years should dim your memory
> Or tears in your eyes should glisten;
> Read again these, my words to you,
> The wind may call my name if you should listen.
>
> For if the world takes you from me,
> My life, my dreams, will surely cease to be;
> And I shall walk again, alone,
> Along the shores of the windswept sea.

Later when he returned to his room he put the poem into an envelope and scrolled across the front, "To you, dear heart. From Doug." He then went across the hall to an office the agents had set up. "I'd like this delivered to my wife," he told the two men sitting there.

"No problem, Colonel," the older man said. "We'll take care of it."

"Anything new on the case?" he asked.

"Yes there is, Colonel, but the Chief will have to fill you in. He'll be back soon."

"Thanks, I'll be in my room."

About an hour later J C Wesley came in. "Well, Colonel, there's been some news fed to us on this case. They tracked down two men who were involved in the shooting. They had them cornered, when the suspects started a small war on the arresting officers, ending up with both of them being killed. That's sure not the way the Chief wanted it, but sometimes it happens. They had learned enough to know for sure these two were just paid killers and it's a certainty there was, in fact, a conspiracy to keep you from testifying."

"Hell," Doug cut in, "there's only one man who stands to lose anything through this mess, and that's Senator Zimm."

"No, that's not really true from all we know at this point," Wesley answered. "You see, there's not a damn thing that points to him. Oh, it's easy to suspect; but it's a lot tougher to make things stick. Now that the two killers are dead, we're to take you back to Washington tomorrow night. Someone wants this hearing to get started and as soon as possible."

"Well, suppose it is the Senator?" Doug asked.

"He can always hire another hit man."

"Well, whoever it is, after botching the job up the first time, they would be insane to try it again, and besides, you will still be under complete protection."

"Well, I hope you guys know what you're doing," Doug said with a smile.

When they arrived in Washington, the agents took Doug directly to the hospital where he spent the day sitting by the bed where his wife lay unconscious. Every doctor that came into the room introduced himself and tried to present an optimistic view of his wife's condition, but as Doug sat holding her hand, he thought how fragile life is, at best. How devastating it is when you must watch a loved one slip away. The longer he sat by her bed watching her, the more he blamed himself for this tragedy. If he had just said "no" when he was asked to go public about the war incident, none of this would have happened. He stood up to leave just as a nurse came in. As he started out the door, he again turned and looked back at Lowie, and then he looked to the nurse. His voice wavered as he softly said, "If my wife doesn't make a complete recovery, there's no way in this world I'll ever forgive myself."

"She will, Colonel, the doctors are sure she will, and very soon now," the nurse said. "So please try and not worry. Everything's going to be all right." He just nodded and went out the door.

The next morning, he was ushered into a conference room in the Pentagon. Sitting around a large table were eight Air Force officers. There was an air of tension in the room. A General stood up and asked Doug to come into the room and take the chair at the end of the long conference table. "Please be seated, Colonel," he said. "Now then, I want you to meet my staff. I personally picked these men for this assignment. I've known them all for many years and I can assure you they all share my concern that you, Colonel Stewart, are treated fairly in this upcoming hearing. We want to establish all the facts before they bring in the wolves. So now, Colonel, please review with us, and start from your last mission which as I understand, was as fighter escort on a bombing raid."

"That's correct, Sir," Doug answered. He tried to relate to the officers in the room the complete mission, step-by-step. After about half-an-hour of talking, he had given them an accurate picture of what had taken place that day.

"Colonel, I don't mean to cast suspicion on your story," the officer at the far end of the table said, "but how can you be so sure the plane that opened fire on you was indeed piloted by Senator Zimm, considering all that had happened that day? Could it be possible you were just assuming the plane was one of ours, and that Zimm was flying it?"

"Well, Major, let me explain it this way. I was the Squadron Leader and it was standard procedure to mark the aircraft of your squadron in some way as to make easy identification of the planes assigned to your squadron. Our marking was a big red bar running at an angle down the vertical tail section and this was quite easy to spot on the ground or in flight. Major, the first thing I did was what we all did in that war; identify our enemy. The enemy at that moment was one of my own planes. Unless Zimm switched planes with someone else while in flight, that pilot was Zimm, for there was no doubt that plane was assigned to him, and it had been his for months. When you are a squadron leader, you're like a mother hen. They might all look alike, but you know which ones belong to you."

After a long pause, the General stood up, looked around at the other officers and said, "Well men, that about does it for this hearing. I do want to tell you, Colonel Stewart, Senator Zimm is still in the reserves and he holds the rank of full Colonel. It's my opinion, if this matter goes beyond a subcommittee hearing, it will probably be handled by a military court. If you haven't as yet, I would suggest you acquire legal assistance."

Just then the telephone located next to the General started flashing. He listened a moment and then said, "Colonel Stewart, now I have some good news for you. Your wife has regained consciousness and is doing very well. They suggested you come to the hospital as soon as possible. You're now dismissed. I'll call my driver to take you there right away."

"Thank you Sir," Doug said. "I really appreciate this. It's the best news I'll ever receive. I'll get back to you tomorrow, but right now, I must leave."

"Take all the time you want, Colonel, this other matter can wait. Being with your wife can't."

By the time he arrived at the hospital, Lowie had been conscious for nearly twelve hours. She was back on solid nourishment and was talking at length with the doctors and nurses. Her latest x-rays showed no internal head injuries and the swelling was completely gone. The doctors and nurses involved in her recovery were all in her room when Doug entered. There was an air of excitement and happiness filling the room. When she saw Doug enter, she raised her outstretched arms and with a big smile said, "Hi, honey." He leaned over and held her in a tight embrace for a long time. By now everyone had left the room. "I've been so frightened and worried about you, I can't tell you how relieved I am to see you smiling again. It was just plain hell without you."

"Sorry to have worried you so much, but honest, I'm okay. I feel wonderful. I really do. In fact, they say I can leave very soon. Everyone here has been wonderful to me, but now, I just want to go home."

"Me too," Doug whispered, and he kissed her again. A few days later they were home again, and their lives had returned to normal. They had long talks about what had happened and it was obvious they both were concerned about what was to take place in the near future.

It was nearly three weeks, before the senate subcommittee hearing began. Doug was notified to report to Washington at nine o'clock, Monday morning. As he entered the room, he was met by a man who introduced himself as Steve Foller, an attorney and a friend of Colonel Broder. They talked a few moments about the hearing and Foller explained this first hearing would be just to outline what the follow-up hearings would cover. Doug was introduced to the committee and then was asked to state for the record, what his case was about. This he did, and shortly thereafter, the hearing was adjourned.

The next meeting of the inquiry was scheduled for Wednesday at 0900. Doug's attorney spent several hours each day with him. They covered every facet of the incident and by Wednesday, Mr. Foller was quite confident their case was solid. The first day was easy for Doug. He was asked to tell in his own words, just exactly what had happened up to the day of his last raid. The committee members were made up of both Democrat and Republican members and being a very hot political as well as military issue, there was concern for both sides of the aisle. Since Zimm was a heavy favorite to win the presidency and keep the current party in power, the two parties had great interest; but for entirely different reasons. The hearing had been in session about an hour when a few in the committee didn't like the way the questioning was being directed. One member asked Doug what he remembered with regard to his stay on the island. "That's hard to answer," Doug replied. "At this point, it's still quite confusing."

"Well then," the man shot back, "isn't it quite possible any of your recollections from thirty years ago would be a lot of guesswork?"

"Sir, I have no problem with my memory about what happened before that Jap hit me on the head with a 2" x 4" board," Doug quickly answered.

"Now, now, Colonel," another member interrupted, "it's obvious you harbor a lot of animosity and prejudice towards the Japanese people, but let me bring you up to the modern world on this point. We do not – and I repeat – DO NOT refer to them as 'Japs'. They are our allies and you will respect them as such." Doug sat like a stone, silently glaring at the man. Again the room grew silent. Finally the man said, "I have no further questions." Other members continued to fire questions at Doug. He deliberately took longer and longer to answer them. The members of the committee from the opposite party were building a case for their colleague, Senator Zimm. Finally, Doug interrupted the questionings with a calm, deliberate voice. "Mr. Chairman, I came here under the assumption this was to be a subcommittee hearing, but I now find myself in what more closely resembles a criminal court proceeding. I wonder if you could clarify my position on that point?"

"I'm inclined to agree with you," one member said, "and I apologize for some of my fellow members here. Gentlemen, we're here to collect information, not to act as judge and jury. This hearing is adjourned until tomorrow at 10 A.M. Thank you, Colonel Stewart."

The next day, they completed their inquiry as far as Doug was concerned. Zimm was to appear the following day. The news media was out in full force by the time Senator Zimm arrived. He smiled and waved to everyone as he hurried inside. They were all shouting questions to him, trying for a comment on his guilt or innocence. Just before he entered the door, he turned and said, "Ladies and gentlemen, I'm innocent of all these ridiculous charges, and the courts will prove that." Shortly after the hearing started, it was obvious the committee was reluctant to ask the Senator any hard questions. All they wanted was some sort of a statement from him, and he was quick to oblige. "Gentlemen, let me assure you, I feel as everyone does concerning Colonel Stewart. I'm very sorry he had to endure what he claims he has; but his misfortune has nothing to do with me. I know it's not popular to call a war hero a liar; but if he continues with these ridiculous charges against me, he leaves me no choice." After about half-an-hour of discussion, the hearing was adjourned.

On his way out, the Senator was again confronted with a mass of reporters; all shouting questions at once. Senator Zimm raised his hands and asked for silence. He wanted to make a statement. He began with, "Members of the press corps; the hearing is over and as soon as the testimony is thoroughly examined, you all will know and realize I'm innocent of all these accusations. I'm very pleased and happy this affair is over and now, if the opposition party doesn't come up with any more mud to sling or dirty tricks, I'll get on with my campaign, and next year at this time we'll all be in the White House, holding our news conferences." Most of the reporters started to laugh and applaud. Zimm was still smiling and waving as he entered his limousine.

The next morning, Doug and Lowie were watching the news and every channel was using their entire time slot on this story. Some were nearly hostile towards Doug. There were some reporters suggesting maybe Colonel Stewart had his own political ambitions. As one reporter said, "What better way to become a household name for free?"

Doug looked at his wife and smiled, "And they think I'm crazy!"

"Dear," she said, "let them say whatever they want. We both know the truth and, in the end, that will all come out."

"I hope you're right."

The next day, Doug reported back to the base and resumed his duties. Nearly three weeks passed before he received any word from Washington. Colonel Broder called and informed him what had developed to date. The subcommittee had evaluated all the information they had compiled on the case and because both principals in the case were still in military service, Doug, being on active duty; and the Senator, an active reserve officer, the case would be handed over to the military courts. "Those politicians want out from under this one," Colonel Broder said. "We here, at the Pentagon, knew this is the course this case would take, and we have been making all the arrangements. We're not going to let this thing develop into a circus."

"Glad to hear that," Doug said. "Let's get this show on the road and get it over with. You people listen to the facts, make a decision, and whatever the verdict, I'll accept it."

"Don't worry Doug," Colonel Broder told him, "there'll be no political pressure in our court. The facts will be determined and the chips will fall where they may."

"Thank you Colonel, that sounds good to me."

"Now Doug, the court proceedings won't start until the fifteenth of next month. That will give you both time to prepare your case with your attorneys. No one will be contacting you again, and I'll see you in court at 0900 on the fifteenth."

"Okay, I'll be there."

The next few weeks, Doug and his friend Bosler spent a lot of time with their attorneys. As the day approached, attorney Foller was quite confident with the material he had prepared. Their case was solid, but he warned them both it might get very dirty; especially, for Doug. The opposition, he was sure, would harp on his mental stability. "Colonel," he said, "fighting this guy in court will be harder than trying to keep him on the job when he was in your squadron during the war."

"Yeah!" Bosler interrupted, "But this time, we're not on some godforsaken island, and we're going to put some pressure on Senator Zimm. We know he's responsible for the hell Doug went through, and I don't want a son-of-a-bitch like that in our White House."

"Hey! I'm on your side," Foller said. "I never liked the windbag myself, and I don't have the valid reason you fellows have. Now, on the murder attempt on you and your wife; I've run into some dead ends, but I have a good man working with the police on that. It could have been a couple of crackpots, but I doubt that. It was too well planned."

"I think we all know who was behind that attempt," Bosler said.

"Yeah, I know," he continued, "without proof, I have to keep my mouth shut."

Foller just smiled. "Now, don't get impatient, Bosler. We'll get all the truth out. It'll just take a lot of work and time."

Their meeting lasted another hour and finally Foller said, "Okay, fellows, I think we're ready to go to court. I'll meet you both at 9 A.M. on the fifteenth. So go home and get some rest, and don't worry. I have a lot of good back-up help working with me on this case. We're going to have a few surprises for Senator Zimm and his boys."

When the day arrived for the hearing, Doug tried to discourage his wife from attending, but she was very insistent. "Honey, are you sure you want to hear this garbage? His lawyers are going to try to shoot me down. For one thing, I'm sure they're going to try to make me look like a lunatic. The longer the case is argued, the dirtier it will get; and I don't want you to get hurt."

"Dear, I won't get hurt, I'll just get mad."

"Well, I wish you would reconsider."

"No, honey, I want to be with you."

"If that's the way you want it, let's go and get it over with."

When they arrived the next morning, the halls were already

filled with reporters. Two MPs escorted them into a room adjacent to the hearing room. Because of Doug's rank, all members of the panel were Colonels and the senior officer was a Brigadier General. When Doug's attorney arrived, Lowie asked if she would be allowed in the hearing room. Foller shook his head, "No. I'm sorry, Mrs. Stewart, this case will fall under Article 32 and that means it will be closed to all personnel except the military who are directly involved."

"You mean I must sit in this room and wait through all this?"

"I'm sorry, Mrs. Stewart, maybe it won't take that long to get through it." She walked to the door with her arm around Doug. He leaned over and kissed her.

"I shall, you know?"

"What?" he smiled.

"I shall wait for you here. Love you," she whispered. "Good luck."

The first hearing before the panel was spent establishing the ground rules to be followed through the court proceedings and allowing both the prosecution and defense to present their cases. The court was then adjourned until 1000 the following day. As Doug came out the door, he was met by a barrage of cameramen and news reporters, all shouting questions and trying to get him to stop and talk. He pushed his way into the room where his wife was waiting. "How did it go, honey?"

"Come on," Doug answered, "let's find a back door out of here. It's like a carnival out there in the hall." They made their way into another hall where a security guard escorted them out to where the cars were parked. They hurried into their car, locked the doors, and drove out of town as fast as possible.

After driving quite some distance, they stopped at a small restaurant. While they waited for their dinner, Doug explained what had taken place in the hearing room. "The first session was nothing more than a lot of review. Now that everyone involved has a fair picture of what this is all about, the real fireworks will begin," he told her.

"Now, Mr. Bosler, just for the record, I'd like to review your account of what happened on the return flight of the last mission Colonel Stewart and you were on together," Attorney Foller stated. "Please tell the panel in your own words just what happened."

Bosler paused a moment and then started to tell his story. "We were ordered to fly fighter support for a bombing mission on an oil-supply dump. When Captain Stewart briefed us on the mission, it was obvious our Squadron Commander was very concerned about our vulnerable position. Because of the distance we had to fly in order to rendezvous with the bombers, there was definitely going to be a fuel problem. Our Captain argued over this aspect of the mission. He tried to reason with our superiors, but the stage had been set and it was vital the oil be destroyed. They said they were sympathetic, but they could not yield; so we had to go. I remember he told us all; fly a straight line, don't get off course, and save your fuel, or we would be going for a swim."

"He meant you would run out of fuel?" the attorney asked.

"Yes," Bosler replied.

"Go on, Sir."

"Well, we accomplished our mission. We lost a few planes; but overall, the raid was well executed. Coming back to our base we had separated from the bombers and were taking an inventory of our damages we had incurred. Some had no damage. Just the fuel supply worry. I had settled in to my position which was next to Captain Stewart's plane as his wingman. I called him and explained I was having trouble with my engine overheating. He ordered me off his wing position and instructed me to gain as much altitude as I could, under my condition. This, he explained, would help me make it home if my engines continued to overheat."

"And how would this help?" the attorney asked.

"Well, every minute I was in the air, the closer to home base I could get; and if I could coax my craft close, I could always throttle back a little; lower the nose a bit, and make a long, slow glide. Seemed like a good idea to me, so that's why I was so much higher than Doug's plane. The weather was good, but there were a lot of broken cloud layers. We had flown for quite some time and I was able to keep Captain Stewart's plane in sight. My engine overheat problem was helped by the higher altitude. I was becoming more confident I could make it back to home base. Suddenly I noticed another of our P-38s trailing the Captain. I could see it quite well below me. I looked around to see whether any more of our guys were closing in; but at that time, we were the only ones. I looked down again and yelled out loud 'My God, No!'. The other P-38 was on the Captain's tail with all guns firing. He was trying to shoot Doug down! Then, I guess the Commander realized what was happening and tried to maneuver out of range. As the two planes were rolling around, I caught sight of the markings on the P-38 that was in chase. It was Zimm. I started to scream and swear as I saw the Captain's plane go into a steep spiral, with smoke trailing out. There was nothing I could do with two sick engines. My only hope was to stay where I was and hope Zimm didn't spot me."

"Now Mr. Bosler, when you say 'Zimm', do you mean Senator Zimm sitting in this court room?"

"Yes, I do."

"And you're sure this is the same man?"

"I'm positive," Bosler answered, as he glared at Senator Zimm.

"Thank you, Mr. Bosler. That will be all for now."

Next, the attorney asked for Mr. Montgomery to take the stand. "Now, Sir," the attorney asked, "I understand you were one who made it back to base."

"Yes Sir," Montgomery answered.

"And would you tell us what you found when you returned?"

"Well Sir, everyone was standing around watching for the planes to come back. Those that were damaged, naturally got priority, and of the few of us that made it back, nearly all had some damage.

"All the fellows were asking if I saw Captain Stewart and Bosler. Everyone wondered if they were going to make it back. Lutz and I were flying close together, most of the way. I had more damage than Lutz and he told me he would fly shot-gun for me the rest of the way back."

"Just what do you mean 'shot-gun'?" Foller asked.

"Well that meant if we encountered any enemy craft, he would try to draw the fire to protect me, since my plane was crippled worse than his."

"Did anyone examine Senator Zimm's plane on return?"

"Yes Sir. After he got out of his plane, he acted very arrogantly, and when I tried to ask him about the raid, he told me to go to hell. He got into the jeep, and drove back to his quarters. Some of us fellows walked over to his plane. It was in perfect shape. We all agreed he had too much fuel on board to have flown in the whole mission like we did."

"How do you explain that, Mr. Montgomery?"

"Simple. He did what he always did. As soon as we

encountered the enemy, he ran and hid; letting the rest of us do the fighting. If he could find a cloud formation, he always managed to get back of it, and that would be the last we would see of him until we got back; and this time was no different. He ran someplace, leaned out his fuel, throttled back the engines, and just waited for the guys to head back to the base. I think it must have been just an accident; him running up on Captain Stewart's back. Then, I guess, he saw a great opportunity. All he had to do was wipe the Commander out, and no one could put in any bad reports on him. In his part of the raid, it was just Captain Stewart, Lieutenant Bosler, and himself. Apparently, he never did see Bosler. So the stage was set to wipe out any bad evidence. Captain Stewart found out early that Zimm's dad was a Senator with a lot of clout. He sent his son over there just to go through the motions and trump up a war record. He had his eye on the White House for little 'Junior'. Well, I'm here to tell you, the mission to the White House is going to be a lot tougher than any he has had so far," Montgomery growled. "What he did is a crime and it scares me to think a man like that is trying to be our President." Senator Zimm leaned over and said something to his attorney. They both smiled.

"Now, Mr. Montgomery," the attorney continued, "when you and your friends checked the plane Zimm was flying, was there any ammunition left?"

"No Sir, all his ammo was gone; but that wasn't unusual. He never returned with any left; even when we knew he didn't engage the enemy at all."

"How do you know that for certain?"

"Well, most everyone knew it. It was a standing joke with his ground crew. They never had to repair damage, but they sure loaded a hell of a lot of ammo."

"Who was his crew chief at that time?"

"I don't recall for certain; I believe it was a Sergeant Gunther." Then as if trying to remember, he continued, "…but on this point, I can't be positive at this time." Then, as the attorney turned towards the panel members, he stated, "It's not really important; but for the record, his name was, in fact, Sergeant Luther Gunther. We have contacted him, and if need be, he will appear before this panel. Next to Captain Stewart, Sergeant Gunther had to work closer to Zimm than anyone else in the squadron. We have talked to him and he has confirmed many of the incidents being reviewed before this panel." The General nodded his head in recognition to that statement.

There were nearly six hours of testimony, with one adjournment for lunch, before the panel finally adjourned to resume the proceedings the following day. Doug's attorney had received word from still another member of the squadron that had served under Doug. This one was former Lieutenant Connors, who lived in Oklahoma City. Neither he nor Montgomery had stayed in service, after the war.

After another day of testimony, Connors confirmed everything Montgomery had stated, and even added new aspects to the charges against Senator Zimm. Finally, the attorney called Doug to the stand. By now the newspapers and TV were jammed with bits and pieces of the story that had leaked out; some true, but most just speculation. Some editorials were bluntly frank about their distrust of an airman being lost for nearly thirty years and then all of a sudden coming out with a political bombshell this close to an election. Many were claiming it was nothing more than a contrived political backlash, with the opposition party grabbing at straws, trying to stop the nearly certain landslide victory for Senator Zimm and the Presidency.

Doug's attorney asked him to start his testimony at the time Lieutenant Zimm joined his squadron. Doug's description of those early accounts only confirmed all the testimony that had been previously given. His attorney guided the questioning in such a way as to compel Doug to go into even more detail of those accounts. At one point the attorney asked Doug if, at any time, he had doubts that the plane firing on him was Lieutenant Zimm.

"No Sir," he replied. "I was sure it was one of ours and it was Zimm's craft."

"How could you be so certain?"

Doug went on to explain the squadron markings and he continued, "Lieutenant Zimm had painted a large red feather, with a curl on the end, on the fuselage pod. It was a symbol of his college-day fraternity house or something. As I maneuvered to avoid his fire, I saw it clearly several times."

"Did you attempt to establish radio contact?"

"No Sir. My radio was damaged and was inoperative."

After continuing with the testimony, Doug's attorney finally thanked him and said, "No further questioning." The panel called for an adjournment until 0900 the next day.

The next day Bosler was called to the stand first. Senator Zimm's attorney started with a rapid-fire line of questioning. He wanted to know his age now; his age at the time of the alleged incident; how long he knew Stewart; how close they were as friends; whether his opinions were influenced by his wing commander; and just what he knew of Senator Zimm at the time, or had he, in fact, known nothing about him? Had he just followed Captain Stewart on missions, being constantly told what to do and how to think? And wasn't it a fact, to this day, he had difficulty determining what is fiction or fact? He gave Bosler no time to respond, but kept hammering away at how poor his memory was of recent events. So how could this panel possibly believe this witness can recall events that he alleged happened back in World War II? With no opportunity to answer the attorney, Bosler was noticeably irritated. He looked at Doug and just shook his head. Finally, he looked at the General who was sitting at the end of a long table. "Don't I get a chance to say anything?" he asked.

"Of course you will, Sir," the General answered.

"Well, I want it known," Bosler fired back, "Captain Stewart was first my Squadron Commander; and then my friend, in that order."

Zimm's attorney interrupted. "We are not interested in your wild-west philosophies," he shouted. "Try to remember you are not out in Idaho at this time! You are here in our nation's capital, but if you can't cope, we can excuse you from this hearing and you can go back to tending your sheep; or whatever you do out there!"

"I object!" Doug's attorney shouted.

"Objection sustained," the General answered. "Now, counsel, I must warn you not to badger the witness."

The attorney looked at Senator Zimm and smiled. "No further questions at this time," he said. He walked back to his chair; sat down, and whispered something to Zimm. They both smiled. There was a short recess and then Zimm's attorney called Connors to the stand. His line of questioning was the same, using tactics so abusive that at times, the General had to intervene. He kept hammering away at how much time had elapsed since this alleged incident took place and just what sort of award were they to receive for their contribution to this scam of discrediting a presidential candidate? Connors remained very calm through all the questions.

Eventually he was able to make it clear to everyone, his only concern was to see justice served in this case. The hearing continued for several more hours and then there was an adjournment until the next day.

That evening Doug and Lowie went for a walk. He didn't tell his wife, but he knew their security men would never be out of sight. With this in mind, he suggested they not go any further than the old Reservoir Park. As they sat down on a bench, Doug looked around to make sure the men were close by. They were. After talking for a while about the day's hearing, Doug asked if she had thought about her tourist business; as to whether she wanted to continue with it or not.

"I don't know for sure, honey, but I don't think I want it anymore. It was great, those years I was active in it, but now I want to stay close to your job. I guess I just want to help you."

"That sounds great to me, but any time you feel you want to go back to it, we can always work things out."

"I know, love," she said, "but I want my life with you more." She thought a while and then said, "You know, the loneliest moment in my life was one night aboard the cruise ship after we left Port Moresby. We were heading up through the Solomon Islands and it was about ten o'clock at night. We were having a forties and fifties music night and some of our old songs were being played, when they got to 'Something to Remember You By', I had to walk out on deck. I just couldn't take it. I stood by the rail for a long time looking out over the sea and I knew then why I was so driven to make the cruise. I wanted to see the part of the world I had lost you to. It was so quiet and peaceful then, and I tried to imagine how much noise and destruction there was all around you, month after month; right there, probably in the very area we were sailing in and I remember saying to myself, 'Oh Doug, if you could only be with me and see how beautiful it is now.' Robin joined me later and we stood by the rail and talked about you for a long time. I finally took the corsage she had given me at the start of the party, and as I threw it into the sea, I said, 'Goodbye Dear Heart. I love you so much. May God be with you, wherever you are.' Robin and I both started to cry. I tried to be brave. I told her everything must come to an end. That was the only time I really tried to let go of our love. But deep down, I knew I never could let go."

Doug stood up, pulling her to her feet. They embraced for a

long time. His eyes were blurred with tears as he whispered, "Thank you God, for keeping her for me." They walked arm in arm back to their home.

The following morning as Doug arrived at the hearing he knew it would be his turn on the stand. This time the questioning would be done by the defense. He was prepared for a grueling ordeal, but he never suspected that there were forces at work to totally destroy him as well as his wife. The attorney started the questioning with much of the same tactics he had used on the other witnesses. Only now it was more evident he was determined to break Doug. His aim was to prove Doug was a mental case to be held in pity, but nothing more.

"Colonel Stewart," the attorney shouted, "isn't it true you have had political ambitions of your own for many years, but because of your background and inability, it is impossible for you to win any offices? Even the much maligned dog catcher?"

With that, Doug leaned back in his chair, looked him straight in the eyes, smiled, and quietly said, "No way, professor, I'm a pilot. That's all I ever wanted to be – and that's what I am."

"Well then Colonel," the attorney said with bitter resentment in his voice, "isn't it true that for nearly thirty years, your brilliant mind was on complete furlough?"

"If that's your description of amnesia, I would have to say 'yes'."

"If you can't remember what happened for thirty years, how can you expect us to believe you can remember anything accurately?"

"I guess that's what we're trying to prove here today," Doug answered.

"Well Colonel Stewart, you went into great detail trying to explain to us how you were so sure the plane that fired on you was flown by Lieutenant Zimm. How do you know that was not a Japanese pilot in a captured American aircraft?"

"I knew my squadron markings and also I was very familiar with my pilots and their aircraft decorations. It's very unlikely these could all be duplicated since none of my squadron aircraft fell into enemy hands."

"But you must admit, it could be possible."

"I suppose it could be – but…"

"Just answer 'yes' or 'no'," the attorney cut in. There was a long silence.

The General looked at Doug. "You will have to answer his questions." More silence.

Finally Doug said, "Yes."

"Now, Colonel, let's get back to some of the statements you made earlier. You condemned then-Lieutenant Zimm for not following orders. If this is true, would you mind telling us if you ever filed an insubordination charge against him?"

"No, I did not."

"Why did you not file one?"

"Well, I never filed one on anyone. I always felt it was better when a problem came up, to settle it within the squadron."

"Wouldn't it be more accurate to say you had no grounds for such a report?"

"No, that is not accurate," Doug snapped back.

"Well Colonel, let's come up to more recent events. When did you first realize the war was over?"

"When I was at Walter Reed Hospital."

"And what's the last thing you recall when you were on the island?"

"I was trying to repair my aircraft with the aid of a Jap Sergeant. There were two other Japs who were put to work on a tower they wanted to use for signaling any ships that might go by. I think one of them hit me on the head with a 2" x 4" and from then, until recently, I couldn't remember anything."

"Well, then, it would be accurate to say for nearly thirty years you have suffered from mental illness?"

"You can call it whatever you want. I don't know if you are a doctor, but I know I'm not mentally ill." With that, some of the panel members smiled. The defense attorney was insistent on directing the questions on Doug's mental stability. After a long and grueling day of cross-examination, the panel called for an adjournment.

When Doug arrived home he found two FBI men waiting for him. He invited them in and immediately they started to check for listening devices. After being certain the room was not bugged, they told Doug and Lowie what their assignment was. Doug would be under protective custody and they were moving his wife up to the Bar Harbour House for protection. They had uncovered another plot on their lives to be implemented on the outcome of the trial, providing Senator Zimm was found guilty.

"When do I have to leave?" Lowie asked.

"Right away," the agent said.

"Oh, no, not again!"

"Yes Ma'am," he said apologetically. "Please pack the things you'll need as soon as possible. I'm sure you won't be detained long."

"I certainly hope not."

When she was ready to leave, the agents took her bags to the car.

Doug held her a long time and then whispered, "I'm sorry I got you into all this, dear heart, I'm truly sorry."

"It's not your fault, honey, it's that damn Zimm, and besides, we're in it together."

Doug kissed her again. "You go up to Bar Harbour and take it easy. As soon as this decision is handed down, I'll meet you up there. We have to sit down and talk about our future. I've been doing some thinking along those lines. Come on, I'll walk you to the car."

The military tribunal dragged on for three more days; when finally both attorneys rested their case. It was up to the panel to make their decision. Everyone was called in at 1000, the following day. A hush fell over the room as the General stood up. He looked towards Senator Zimm and then towards the panel. "After due process of the military court, we find the defendant guilty as charged, for the attempted murder of Douglas Stewart during wartime military service.

"You will now stand and face this panel, as your sentence is read aloud for your part in this crime."

As Zimm stood up, he turned towards the panel holding a revolver in his right hand. He began to shout, "You have left my political career in shambles, but you will not humiliate me any further." With that he fired four shots at the panel; then quickly turned the weapon on himself. Putting the barrel in his mouth, he pulled the trigger again! There was a muffled explosion as he fell to the floor, dead. The whole courtroom was in panic. Two of the judging panel were wounded critically. Doug motioned to Bosler who was closest to him to get out the side door. When they came out the door, the hall was jammed with newsmen, all yelling questions about the gunshots; and asking if anyone was killed. Doug kept pushing Bosler towards the door to the parking lot.

Once outside, they both ran to Doug's car. Within minutes they were several blocks away from the chaotic scene! Doug started for the freeway at a high speed. Neither said anything for quite a while. Finally Bosler said, "Where are we going?"

"We're getting the hell out of this town," Doug answered. "No telling who might be shooting at us next."

They spent the rest of the day and that night in a motel, north of Washington. They kept watching the news on TV as the story was being pieced together. The news media was going crazy. The Senator was dead; there were two men in the hospital in critical condition; two of the witnesses had disappeared; and the presidential election was in shambles. "How long are we going to hide?" Bosler asked.

"I'll call Colonel Broder in the Pentagon tomorrow morning. The smoke should be cleared by then."

The next morning Doug called Colonel Broder's office. "Is the Colonel in?" he asked the secretary.

"Yes, he is. Who should I say is calling?"

"Colonel Stewart."

"Oh, Colonel, just a moment. He's been trying to contact you."

"Doug? This is Colonel Broder. Are you okay?"

"Yeah. I'm okay. Bosler and I are here in a motel north of town. What's our next move?"

"Well, Doug, go to the airport. I'll meet you there at the main gate. We have a plane standing by. Tell you all about it when we get there." And he hung up.

About an hour later they were sitting in Colonel Broder's limousine. "Now this is what I want you to do, Doug. Fly up to our compound at Bar Harbour where we have your wife. You two can have a little vacation at our expense for a while. As for you, Mr. Bosler, we are arranging a flight to take you back home. Now you both will be under our protection for a while, until we're sure there is not a conspiracy of any kind going on."

They talked quite a while about the turn of events and when it came time to leave, Doug slapped Bosler on the back, saying, "Old Buddy, thanks for everything, and some time soon my wife and I will be out to see you. Maybe we can go out and have a few laughs once."

"Okay, Colonel, I'll be looking forward to it."

It was late afternoon when Doug arrived at Bar Harbour. A car was waiting and in a few minutes he was at the beach house where Lowie was staying. "Your wife is down on the beach," the agent said. "There's steps behind the house you'll have to use. It's the only way to get down over the cliff."

"Okay," Doug shouted, as he ran out of the back door. When he got to the steps, he could see Lowie far below, walking near the water's edge. The sun was now quite low in the sky and the air was very cool. He stood there a few moments watching her. The seagulls were all around her; the sky was turning dark gray, with streaks of gold stabbing through. He thought it looked just like a picture postcard.

He was nearly to the bottom of the steps when she turned around and saw him. She screamed in delight and waved both arms in the air; then started running to him. He threw his arms around her, picked her up and spun her around the ring several times. She was laughing and crying at the same time. They had to shout because of the roar of the sea.

"I love you, love you, love you," Doug shouted. "And from now on, we'll do whatever you want to do. So tell me, honey, what do you want to do with the rest of our lives?"

She squeezed him as hard as she could and, looking up with tear-filled eyes, she smiled and said, "Just be with you, my dear heart. Forever."

ISBN 1425110746